THE AUNTS

BY THE SAME AUTHOR

FICTION

The Almond Tree
An Object for a Walk
The Deep End
The Gantillons
Kind Relations
The Last Enchantments
The Rivers of Babylon
Stepsons
Unreal City
Watering-Place

NON-FICTION

Aegean Greece
Byzantium and Istanbul
Cavafy: A Critical Biography
Mainland Greece
The Morea
The Novels of George Eliot
The Novels of Ivy Compton-Burnett
The Novels of Jane Austen
Some Principles of Fiction
A Treatise on the Novel
Elizabeth and Ivy (Peter Owen)

Robert Liddell

THE AUNTS

PETER OWEN · LONDON

ISBN 0 7206 0665 9

PETER OWEN PUBLISHERS
75 Kenway Road London SW5 0RE

First published in Great Britain 1987
© Robert Liddell 1987

Photoset and printed in Great Britain by
Redwood Burn Limited Trowbridge Wiltshire

To

HENRY

En ma fin est mon commencement.

Il ne faut pas seulement avoir la douceur du miel, qui est aromatique et odorant, c'est à dire la suavité de la conversation civile avec les étrangers, mais aussi la douceur du lait entre les domestiques et proches voysins: en quoy manquent grandement ceux qui en rue semblent des anges, et en la mayson des diables.

St François de Sales

Auprès des personnes qu'on aime, le sentiment nourrit l'esprit ainsi que le coeur, et l'on a peu besoin de chercher ailleurs des idées.

Jean-Jacques Rousseau

1

'How lucky it is that people never seem to die at luncheon-time, and want a lawyer or a priest,' said the Revd James Freeling.

'I can't think why they don't,' said his friend Philip Milsom. 'My own vitality is always very low at this hour.'

'Because you don't eat enough breakfast, my dear,' said James. 'All this vain attempt at slimming.'

'Vain in both senses, I'm afraid,' said Philip ruefully. 'But you see, I lead such a sedentary life at the office – not bicycling about a huge parish like you. And if a client wanted to be visited at home, he'd want old Dolmidge to come and change his will, not a whipper-snapper like me.'

For Philip was a partner in an old family firm of solicitors in this inland watering-place. James, his great friend at Oxford, had lately come there as an assistant priest at the Church of St Simon Zelotes, and it was convenient and agreeable for them to lodge together. The time was the autumn of 1938, shortly after the Munich agreement.

Their landlady, Miss Snape, who had only just learned that it was not 'done' to knock – and imperfectly believed it – entered apologetically.

'There's a lad to see you, Father James.'

'What have you done with him?'

'I'm afraid I was very naughty,' said Miss Snape archly. 'I put him in your study to wait till you'd finished lunch.'

'Well, I'd better go and see him at once, I suppose,' said James. 'No rest for the wicked.'

'For the good!' gushed Miss Snape. 'You're far too good to these lads, Father James.'

James returned after a few minutes.

'What did the lad want?' asked Philip.

'A letter for his mother for the Ear, Nose and Throat Hospital. I said I'd get him one. Could you ask your aunts? I'm sure they're subscribers.'

'Why not ask them yourself? It's time I took you to see them.'

'A pity your free day is my busiest day. But I suppose I could just get up to them in time for luncheon, if they wanted me then.' For they lived in a residential district about twenty minutes' walk across the heath.

'Of course they would. You're too important on our horizon to get off with tea, and they don't have guests in the evening.'

'I hope they don't disapprove of me,' said James.

'They hardly could, because of your family,' said Philip. 'A Freeling of Freeling! And you're a clergyman too – even if St Simon's is "a bit too High, even Extreme". It would be irreverent to disapprove.'

'One of your aunts, Miss Elwell I think, comes to high mass, doesn't she?'

'"Sung Eucharist", we call it. At eight o'clock she goes to St John's nearby.'

'And the others?'

'The Keyworths? Oh, Aunt Jane goes to what they call "the choral" at St John's. She'd not even be above going to matins. Uncle George, I fancy, prefers to worship his Maker in the open air – though I'm glad to say he never talks about it – in company with a smelly old dog. That is, when he's well enough.'

'I hope I'll go down all right,' said James modestly.

'Uncle George is sure to like you. His family lived near Freeling before yours sold the place.'

'That's ancient history now.'

'And don't preach "provocative" sermons with Aunt Eliza in church.'

'I'm on at evensong the next two weeks. Does she come then?'

'My dear James, you don't yet understand a place like this. "Nice people" don't go to church in the evenings. They leave it to the servants.'

The next Sunday was chosen, and Philip decided to ring his aunts up at the first proper moment – perhaps when they were finishing tea.

'They aren't yet used to the telephone, though they've had it for fifteen years. One must choose one's time. And like most people who never have any engagements they think they need plenty of notice if you want to suggest anything out of the usual routine.'

'You're funny, Philip,' said James. 'I know you adore them, but you don't talk as if you did – you make them sound such fussy old ladies.'

'But I love them like that. I wouldn't have them different for anything. And I dare say they'd never guess how devoted I am to you from the way I talk.'

'Better not, perhaps,' said James with a smile.

Then there was a knock, since Miss Snape for once had forgotten herself.

'Your auntie's on the telephone, Mr Milsom.'

'I'll go and see,' said Philip.

'Philip, dearest,' said his Aunt Jane. 'Your Aunt Eliza was just saying it was time we asked Mr Freeling to come and see us.'

'And James was just saying it was time he called,' said Philip, not quite accurately.

'Do you think you could bring him to luncheon with you on Sunday?'

'Yes, I'm sure he could come. He could fit it in between services.'

'They have such a lot of them at St Simon's.'

'Well, I'll run and ask him, if you'll hold the line a minute.'

'I am to ask you to luncheon on Sunday,' said Philip. 'I'll say you will come?'

'Oh, I'm glad it was that, Mr Milsom!' said Miss Snape. 'Your aunties are neither of them ones for the telephone, and I was afraid something had happened.'

Philip Milsom and Eliza Elwell returned from church on foot. James, who had had to get out of a vestment, came later on his bicycle. They found Jane Keyworth reading the paper in the morning-room. Presently George, her husband, painfully shuffled into the room. His left hand held a stick, and with the right he was fumbling in an attempt to do up a fly-button without being caught by his wife or his sister-in-law. At once he broke wind. Philip tried to cover this up by introducing James, and then talked to his uncle while his aunts were making conversation with the visitor.

'My dear chap, it's awful having to work out one's movements. I never get used to it,' said George. 'You can't imagine what it is to be unable just to get up or sit down or walk across a room without thinking twice about it – and without being as slow as a tortoise.'

'I can imagine it, just a little,' said Philip. 'I've had a sprained ankle. There were movements one couldn't make without great pain, and some quite simple movements one couldn't make at all. And then there was that time when my back gave all that trouble.'

'Your Aunt Jane really ought to understand better and make more allowances. She's been ill often enough herself. Eliza is as tough as a horse, and never has a thing wrong with her, except her teeth.'

The luncheon bell rang. 'Danny and I will struggle in first,' said George, prodding the old West Highland terrier. 'We're slower than the rest of you.' And he began another painful shuffle.

'*Wenn er allein ist, das tut er nicht,*' murmured Eliza under her breath to Philip.

'I used to go over to meets at Freeling when I was a boy,' said George. 'In the time of Sir Aldebert and Lady Alethea. Were they your grandparents?'

'No, my great-uncle and great-aunt,' said James. 'They hadn't any children, so my father came into the place, and had to sell it.'

'How sorry you must be,' said Eliza.

'Not really,' said James. 'We'd never lived there, and the death duties were ruinous.'

'Sad to see these old places going,' said Jane. 'What is it now?'

'A girls' school. A very good one, I believe. At all events it was too expensive for my sister to be sent there.'

'It does seem a pity,' said Eliza.

'Not to me,' said James. 'The house is perfectly hideous, rebuilt after a fire in 1860. I should hate to be sacrificed to it as younger brothers were in the past. I should be wretchedly off.'

'I'm afraid you're being cynical,' said Jane. 'Money isn't everything.'

'It almost is, if you haven't any,' said Philip.

'I don't know how I should have got through Oxford without my small share,' said James. 'And I could never have travelled.'

Foreign travel – a safe subject for conversation, though George's only contribution was that he was now past it.

James recommended him a French spa, and felt himself frowned upon.

Foreign travel, now so difficult. Of course during the crisis of 1932 one couldn't go abroad; it would have been unpatriotic. Though there was probably no harm in going to the Cape, like that woman over the way, who had money to burn. Germany, of course, was out of the question because of that dreadful Hitler – not that one ever much cared to go there – and one couldn't feel quite the same about Italy any more.

'You mean "the blameless Ethiopians"?' murmured Philip. 'I don't mean to let politics keep me away.'

So sad, one used to admire Mussolini so much, because the trains were on time. One knew a delightful *pensione* in Fiesole, and it was nice staying early in the year at San Remo or Bordighera. Even if the hotel didn't give you tea, there was a very good tea-room near. Poor old Kate Springfield had called her dog 'Musso' (she'd had a Garibaldi before) and now it wouldn't answer to 'Haile Selassie'.

'She might try "Lassie"', suggested Philip, and he was frowned on as if he had committed an irreverence.

Well, perhaps one might soon begin to think of going to Italy again.

Spain was too dangerous. So many of one's friends had liked to go to Malaga in the winter; and now it was in the hands of those horrible Reds. And anyway Spaniards were so cruel to animals.

Where could one go? The South of France was ruined.

'Switzerland?' suggested James.

But that was no good, except perhaps Lugano. You see, it was in late January or early February that one wanted to get away – to break up the long English winter. Though of course we had the best climate in the world, no extremes. The

11

Northern countries had nothing to offer, though otherwise irreproachable.

Greece was said to be still too primitive, and it was such a long sea voyage to Egypt. One knew nothing about North Africa.

'Do you know, I often think people are rather priggish about foreign travel,' said Philip. 'I don't see why people shouldn't go anywhere that's reasonably safe. People talk as if all the money they spend in Italy goes straight into Mussolini's pocket. They forget most of it goes for their board and lodging.'

'I suppose the argument is that if Italian hotel-keepers have a thin time it will make Mussolini unpopular,' said James. 'I don't think much of it as an argument myself. I believe that Italy has been full of tourists all the time.'

'Some people don't like to condone what Italy has been doing,' said Jane, tossing her head.

'Italy must be all the nicer without them,' said Philip. 'I can't stand "some people". They think themselves and their opinions so important, and they enjoy making a show of them.'

'I don't think either of you would be wise to go to Italy just yet,' said Eliza in a quiet, reasonable tone. 'You have your positions here to think of, and people do talk so.'

'Well, by next spring the town will be out of mourning for Abyssinia,' said Philip. 'And I couldn't go before. Meanwhile Miss Springfield is going to give lectures in the Pump Room on Italian painting.'

'Will people go?' said Jane.

'I certainly shall, if I have time,' said Philip.

Eliza remembered that James had said that he liked damsons. 'Let's go into the kitchen garden and get a basketful. But you're on your bicycle?'

'Never mind, I'm sure Philip will bring them,' said James.

But at that moment George gave a cry of pain. Philip was at once at his side.

'Phil, old chap, help me upstairs.'

When they were safely out of hearing George confessed: 'You know, this time I really was putting it on. I don't often, though Eliza thinks I do. I hadn't got a twinge, but I had sprung a leak. I was suddenly taken short. At my age these little accidents happen. Do you think you can smuggle my trousers out to the cleaners?'

'I shouldn't bother, Uncle George. It's just water. There won't be a stain. I'll wash it out and put on the gas fire to dry them. Then I'll help you to bed and say you're tired and want a rest. You don't think Aunt Jane will come up?'

'No fear!' said George.

Philip went down to find James preparing to go.

'Don't forget your damsons, Father Freeling,' said Eliza.

'How stupid you are!' said Jane. 'Mr Freeling is on his bicycle. Philip will take them.'

'Remember to be on time,' said James. 'You're reading a lesson at evensong.'

'You *are* being roped in,' said Jane.

2

'Father Freeling is a nice, simple creature, I thought,' said Eliza. 'He was delighted with the damsons.'

'Mr Freeling? Yes, he's quite a nice young man. Not very gifted, I should say.'

'No, I think Philip is the leading spirit,' said Eliza fondly. 'But I'm sure he likes that.'

'I'm afraid he's rather beginning to lay down the law.'

'Well, after all, it's his profession,' said Eliza. 'But I think Father Freeling is very much attached to him. It's nice to see it.'

'I'm not sure that these intense friendships are quite healthy,' said Jane. 'Philip hardly sees anything of anyone else.'

She had to say something in opposition to her sister. There was no hostility between them, for they needed if they did not love each other. Argument, however, was necessary to them, and almost their only form of conversation. This was indeed a family trait, and rather difficult to exercise because they never talked about religion and both took their politics from the same newspaper. However, where there's a will there's a way, and one can always disagree over people even if one loves them, as they both loved their nephew.

'Philip has to see all sorts of people in his working hours,' said Eliza. 'It must be a comfort to have a friend out of his own world. They've known each other so long – they were at Oxford together, and school before that.'

'But Philip hated school.'

'That might attach him all the more to anyone he'd liked there.'

'Well,' said Jane more graciously, 'I suppose it's not such a bad arrangement for the time being. Though they do live in rather a slum.'

'The neighbourhood has gone down,' Eliza agreed. 'But it's not a bad house. They have good rooms, and for both of them it's conveniently near their work.'

'Miss Snape seems quite a nice little person, and very civil,' said Jane, who had used all her graciousness when she had made a visit of inspection.

'A little what I call "smarmy",' said Eliza.

'I dare say she makes quite a good thing out of the boys,' said Jane. 'But they say she feeds them well, and their things are nicely kept.'

'I liked your aunts,' said James. 'They were so nice to me. Mrs Keyworth was absolutely charming.'

'While I was talking to poor Uncle George.'

'Yes, he didn't get much of a look-in.'

'No, I'm sure he wanted to talk to you about Freeling. Aunt Jane firmly keeps him down, and likes to think it's Aunt Eliza who's doing it.'

'Miss Elwell seems a fine stalwart character.'

'She is,' said Philip. 'But Aunt Jane has the charm – when she likes. You know, she made quite a conquest of Miss Snape.'

'I'm afraid – if you don't mind my saying so – she has rather what St François de Sales calls "the sweetness of honey" for strangers, but not always "the sweetness of milk" at home.'

'I remember your sermons, my dear: "angels in the street, devils at home",' said Philip. 'Well, she's not often really diabolic at home, and oddly enough she's quite sincere when she's being angelic. There's no vanity about it at all, she never thinks about making an effect. She becomes genuinely interested in strangers, and very compassionate. Sometimes, of course, it's quite useless – for example, when she lets herself get too unhappy about things or people in the newspapers.'

'Of course nobody can be so annoying as people at home,' said James.

'No,' said Philip. 'If she had the same temptation to let fly anywhere else, she would let fly. But Aunt Eliza is good all through.'

'They're rather wonderful,' said James, opening a window. 'Like people in Jane Austen.'

'Oh no, James! I thought you were better read! Jane Austen's people were living in their age as contemporaries – some were even a little ahead of their time. One or two of the girls disapproved of the slave-trade, and several people were rather puritan and evangelical.'

'Yes, one easily becomes anachronistic,' said James. 'One forgets that at one time the evangelicals were ahead of other people, and not always by any means old-fashioned.'

'My aunts are old-fashioned,' said Philip. 'More like people in *Cranford*, though not very, if you must make a comparison. They're living in the thirties like us, but as survivors. It's a way of living as much as any other. But they'd *like* to be living in the years between the old Queen's two jubilees. "When Grandpa was alive", and they had the big house in the background.'

'In this century, but not of it,' said James.

'Exactly,' said Philip. 'They belong to "better days".'

'I'm afraid one oughtn't really to say "better days",' said James. 'Think of the abuses of the time, and the life of the poor.'

'Let's be honest, and think of ourselves for the moment,' said Philip. 'For certainly no one else will think of us. And in our professions neither of us is allowed to forget the others for long. Let's say "Better days" – at least between these walls.'

'But oughtn't one then – wouldn't one then have been gnawed by conscience?'

'I doubt it. I think that's another anachronism. Look at all the excellent people who weren't! And if we'd been "serious-minded" we could have comforted ourselves with Tennysonian optimism about the great world spinning for ever down the ringing grooves of change.'

'Yes, I suppose we should have expected the world to become a far better place than anyone can now imagine.'

'And I'm afraid that we – if we live – may come to look back on the thirties as "better days".'

Even in this quiet town there were pubs and clubs where young people (and people not so very young) liked to stand or sit and drink and smoke and talk rather shrilly about 'the condition of England' and the state of the world. They did not – and soon they were proved right – take a very rosy view of it. But they were more pleased with themselves than they had

16

any good reason to be, and appeared to think that they were thus usefully occupied. James had moments when he spoke of their 'social conscience', and he almost felt tempted to join their sessions from time to time. Philip answered him out of the catechism: he was not to covet or desire other men's goods (as most of them did) but to learn and labour truly to get his own living and to do his duty in that state of life unto which it had pleased God to call him.

'But my state of life is so easy, too easy.'

'That isn't for you to say,' said Philip. 'If it was hard, would you have the right to complain? I'm always having to preach your sermons for you.'

At all events they were both agreed that some neutrality about outside subjects best became them, and made them more useful to James's parishioners and Philip's clients than any sort of partisanship. Philip at least was very glad to come to this conclusion.

'Now I've been shown to your family, you ought to be shown again to mine,' said James. 'Let's arrange to have luncheon with them the next time you have business in London. I can easily go up for a day.'

'I haven't seen your parents since they came down to school and took us out,' said Philip. 'I've never been able to tell the aunts much about them. Of course they were interested the other day when you let out that you had a sister.'

'Matchmaking!' said James with a smile. 'You need have no fear of Dora. She's all for athletics and Girl Guides and female friends. A real man-hater. Anyway she wouldn't be likely to be there.'

'Just as well,' said Philip. 'I should have been lengthily examined about her by Aunt Eliza.'

'She'd be the one to do it?'

'Yes, I think she has great forensic talents,' said Philip. 'It will begin: "So you had luncheon with Father Freeling's family. Who do they consist of?" Then one generally has to think how to put the names in order, so as to get off lightly.'

'Why?'

'Oh, there is usually one dangerous name – perhaps more, if there are a lot of people.'

17

'How, dangerous?'

'There are lots of different ways. People can be religiously, socially, politically or morally not quite to be approved of, or they can invite question on other grounds. Then one wonders where to place the dangerous name. Not at the beginning – and certainly not at the end. At the end it would look as if one had made a cowardly attempt to suppress it. But I'm sure you haven't anyone of that sort.'

'It depends who's there. You might meet Uncle Edmund, who's a Jesuit, or Cousin Flora, who's a divorcée. It's not very likely poor Alfred would be there. He's done time – boys.'

'"Fancy inviting you to meet a gaolbird!"' said Philip, in Jane's voice.

'Yes, I can imagine them as being pretty severe,' said James. 'But I do like them. They give me a sort of pointer in life. I'm always hearing about "deprived" or "underprivileged" lads, or others. Sentimental people pretend that it's "Society" that's to blame for the horrid things they do – and horrid they often are. What rubbish! "Society" means your aunts, and they never deprived anyone.'

'Nor underprivileged them either,' said Philip. 'No, it's the lads' fault, their own fault, their own most grievous fault,' he continued. 'My aunts do a lot of good in their quiet way, and support charities, though they're far from rich – and they give secretly to the "genteel poor". I've found that out more than once.'

'And if the lads come from bad homes – which is often far from the case – that's not a thing confined to the lower classes.'

'No, indeed!' said Philip. 'You remember Andrew Faringdon at Oxford, I dare say? He and his brother sometimes come here. They have relations in the place. Well, I've never known anyone with a more ghastly home than they had – and they've turned out all right.'

'Yes, I remember, there was that bitch of a stepmother.'

'Thank God to hear you say that, James! I hate people who say "We mustn't judge", or "Who are we to condemn her?" Well, we're people who haven't bullied defenceless children, whatever else we've done.'

'I think it means that we mustn't judge her degree of guilt,' said James. 'She may be mad.'

'I dare say. But I like the *mot* of Péguy: *Je ne juge pas, je condamne.*'

'We certainly ought to condemn some forms of behaviour.'

'What I really hate are people who say they want to hear the other side. It's moral cowardice disguised as fairness. They're afraid of making a decision. If thugs rape girls or knock men about and rob them, there isn't another side.'

'Yes, it's all very well to talk about "rehabilitation" or "re-education" – though I don't see how one can "re-educate" the uneducated. But there ought to be more talk about repentance and shame, and sorrow for sin.'

'All this stupidity – I don't know who began it – about the misuse of the words "positive" and "negative" and the attempt to equate them with good and evil! We have to say "no" to a lot of things, and the Peace Pledge Union people are quite right to say it to war.'

'Philip, I've just this moment thought of a distinction,' said James. 'I don't know if it will work. I should say your aunts are first-rate moralists. What they say is right or wrong generally *is* right or wrong. But they would not be equally good as penologists, who have to take causes into account – who almost have to examine what cowardly people call "the other side", even if it only exists in a vestigial state.'

'In life, only jurors hear the other side,' said Philip.

'I feel, like jurors, we ought often to recommend mercy,' said James. 'But we may exact repentance as a condition. We ourselves don't expect to be forgiven without it.'

3

'I suppose you get roped in for a lot of parish activities,' said Jane.

'Only Church ones,' said Philip. 'Sometimes I read a lesson, or replace one of the servers who has fallen out.'

'You don't have to help with the boys' club?'

'Oh dear no!' said Philip. 'I don't think James needs any help. He wouldn't like me to go there.'

'How odd!' said Jane. 'Why shouldn't he?'

'Well, I might make him feel self-conscious,' said Philip, rather awkwardly searching for the right thing to say. 'You see, he has to put on another personality for the boys – as a schoolmaster or an actor has to put one on. He can't quite be *my* James – I mean the one I sit opposite to at breakfast.'

'I can see that,' said Eliza. 'I suppose he doesn't like you to hear him preach?'

'That's more impersonal,' said Philip. 'I'd only be one of a sea of faces in front of him, and he wouldn't care. But he's not at all a good preacher.'

'I've only once heard him,' said Eliza. 'He's not often on at eleven o'clock.'

'No, he says the nine o'clock mass as a rule,' said Philip. 'I usually go to that and serve him, and we breakfast after it. Then I go for a walk, and James comes too if he's not wanted at eleven o'clock.'

'It seems rather a happy-go-lucky arrangement,' said Jane. 'And at one time a professional man wouldn't like to be seen going out in the forest on Sunday mornings. It's a step towards the continental Sunday.'

'Well, he's been to church,' said Eliza. 'That's what matters.'

'I suppose, what with his boys' club and other things, Mr

Freeling is out quite a lot,' said Jane. 'You must have a good many evenings by yourself.'

'Not so very many,' said Philip. 'And I never mind that – I always have plenty to do.'

'Papers from the office?' suggested Jane.

'No, I leave all that behind when I go home.'

'Philip has better things to do at home,' said George. 'I hope you're not neglecting your drawing?'

'A hobby is hardly a better thing than one's work,' said Jane, tossing her head. 'His father nearly always brought home work to do in the evening.'

'Poor Gilbert hadn't got Philip's gifts,' said George.

'Just as well for Philip!' said Jane. 'He made the firm what it is. Old Dolmidge didn't do much.'

'So Philip doesn't have to work so hard,' said George. 'He could chuck the whole thing up if he felt like it, and be a full-time artist, not just a weekender.'

'I'm sure he'd never do anything so irresponsible,' said Eliza, pursing her lips. 'Would you, Philip?'

'Not just now, at any rate,' said Philip. 'Not till I've found my feet.'

'But you'd never even think of it?'

'Never is a long day,' said Philip. 'I might. If I ever sold out, I should have enough to live on.'

'Hardly, when you're married and have a family,' said Eliza.

'Who knows?' said George. 'His work might sell.'

'But there wouldn't be a position to hand on to his son,' said Jane. 'And anyway art isn't a solid profession.'

'That's part of its attraction,' said Philip. 'And I don't think I'm the marrying sort.'

'Nonsense, a man has to marry,' said Jane. 'Not that a woman need.'

'Sometimes he's better off single,' said George, with some feeling.

'But the Milsoms are such an old family,' said Eliza. 'You wouldn't like them to die out.'

'They were never anything in particular,' said Philip.

'I thought they were,' said Eliza, in an almost hurt voice.

'One of Father's old cousins had delusions of grandeur,' said Philip. 'I suppose she must have talked to you. But there's

21

nothing in it. We never were anybody, never had a place or a title.'

'Well, that's something for you to start,' said Eliza.

'I have no ambitions that way,' said Philip. 'And, after all, I'm the entire family now – there's no one else to consider.'

'I don't know about that. Your father would have wished the firm and the family to go on.'

'I dare say he would,' said Philip. 'But there will be no living person to care.'

'The wishes of the dead don't matter, I suppose?' said Jane sarcastically.

'I don't think they do,' said Philip. 'It's not as if I had made any promise. I never pretended to Father to care about the firm.'

'Tchah!' said Jane impatiently. 'Bad luck on Gilbert, all the same, if his work is to be thrown away.'

'I'm sure Philip will be a sensible boy,' said Eliza. 'Don't let's cross bridges till we come to them.'

But when Philip had gone, the sisters turned on George.

'You encourage Philip too much about his drawing,' said Jane. 'He's in danger of neglecting his work as it is.'

'He's very talented,' said George. 'He might make art his work. He's already getting known. He's had commissions to design book jackets, and he's illustrating a book at present.'

'It's not a man's work,' said Jane.

'Anything is a man's work if it's done properly,' said George.

'But what will it lead to?' asked Eliza.

'Why need it lead to anything but more work of the same sort?'

'But it won't give him a position,' said Eliza.

'Why should he want a position if he's happy?' said George.

'Is happiness the whole object in life?' said Jane sharply.

'It's a major object,' said George. 'Money is only a means to it, though a very necessary means.'

'There's such a thing as duty,' said Jane, tossing her head.

'To whom?' asked George. 'Philip has no near family but ourselves, and he's a very kind, dutiful nephew.'

'What his father would have said!' exclaimed Jane.

22

'I don't care a button what Gilbert would have said – nor do you or Eliza. He was only an "in-law", like me.'

'A bit more – he was decorated,' said Jane. 'He got the OBE.'

'I nearly made a floater with Aunt Jane,' said Philip. 'She thought you'd want me to help in the boys' club. I said you wouldn't have me there.'

'No,' said James with a smile. 'I'm afraid the sight of the two of us might be a bit too much for the lads. What a good thing neither of us has ever been attracted to the English lower classes!'

'Yes, I confess I sympathize with that character of George Eliot's who thought they were brutes, and hated their accents and their scent and whatnot. I hate their ties and their hair oil and their cigarettes.'

'I dare say George would have, too – from her position near the bottom of the lower middle class. She wasn't much exposed to them. But I am! God, how I hate that part of my job! To be forced into quite close relationship with people for whom one can't get up much sympathy, and who don't talk the same language.'

'I suppose some things are even more boring,' said Philip. 'Signing papers and recommendations and all the formal things you have to do. Rather like the worst chores of my profession.'

'Though with no possible intellectual interest. All the same, I like it better. There are worse things than boredom.'

'And to have to dress up for our horrid work!' said Philip. 'I shall chuck the office and wear what I like – the bother of changing!'

'Well, you change out of your office suit quickly enough.'

'I should think so! My aunts think me very slack because I never wear a stiff collar or a hat, or carry a stick.'

'Or a rolled umbrella!'

'Well, what's the use of the thing if it's rolled? And then dinner, in any house one stays in or visits – to be frowned on unless one wears a boiled shirt.'

'Except on Sundays!' said James.

'Yes, that's a merciful relief. "Be the day weary, be the day

23

long, at last it ringeth to Evensong" – and the cook has gone to it, so it's only supper and not worth dressing for. Almost worthwhile having to eat cold grey roast beef, and beetroot salad, and stodgy chocolate shape!'

'I escape a lot, wearing a cassock most of the time.'

'Yes, but that soutane thing of yours, that doesn't need a dog-collar, isn't very well thought of – rather *Roman*!'

'I dare say the Vicar would like me to wear a blazer when I'm with the lads,' said James. 'But I prefer to keep my distance.'

'I always feel a lot of sympathy with that man in Trollope who thought dressing was a bore, and making calls a bore and – saving your presence – church a bore. Though I don't see why he had to go, living in London as he did.'

'So he very sensibly went to live in Italy,' said James. 'Wasn't he the man who *knew he was right*? And how right he was!'

'You suffer more than I do,' went on James. 'You have to dress up for weddings and funerals, and I don't. How is it you manage not to be *endimanché* when you go to your aunts on Sundays?'

'I'm thought to be keeping Uncle George in countenance. He never is. You saw his old carpet slippers. May God preserve them to him from Aunt Jane!'

'But you know, if we lived in "foreign parts", we might find people even more dressy than here, at least in the daytime.'

'Yes, James, but we should be the "mad English" who are known to be sloppy. And indeed they don't think it much matters what they wear abroad.'

'It's not really very respectful,' said James. 'One wouldn't like to go so far as to offend people.'

'Perhaps not,' said Philip. 'But think of the opposite tradition! Those generals wearing full-dress uniform on the battlefield – those explorers putting on dinner-jackets to eat corned beef in the jungle!'

'And they're thought to have gone native if they give it up,' said James.

'But I'd rather like to receive a formal invitation from a cannibal chief, who'd been to Eton and Oxford, to a dinner of braised missionary with "white tie" put on it in brackets.'

'I might be the *pièce de résistance*,' said James. 'I hope they'd have dressed me nicely.'

24

'One hopes so,' said Philip. 'In life, my dear, you always look better dressed than anyone else when you wear your soutane. I won't say the same for you in trousers. But I have deliberately kept off coming to the point.'

'What is the point?'

'I haven't dared ask you before. Do you feel any shame about our past?'

'So long past!' said James. 'Not now, so far as "human respect" goes. I regret sin *in tantum peccatum* in so far as it was sin, an offence against God, disobedience. But good can come out of evil, and the consequences seem to me entirely good. I have, I hope, contrition, but no remorse.'

'Yes, it has strengthened the tie between us.'

'And we've done no harm to a single human being,' said James. '*Tibi soli peccavi*, we say in the Miserere, and it's literally true.'

'Not that that would prevent "some people" – as my Aunt Jane would say, "such she gives her dreadful daily line to" – from being very unpleasant, and feeling personally affronted.'

'There's no limit to the beastliness of "some people".'

'Aunt Jane would never copy them, but she'd always have a sneaking admiration for them.'

'At one time I feared them,' said James. 'Perhaps one was right to fear them. But I no longer have any scruples about deceiving them.'

'I suppose Aunt Jane thinks they have an austerer code, and higher standards. I own I rather like it when one of them comes a cropper, and it often happens.'

'One ought to grieve, I suppose.'

'But you don't, dearest James, you don't!'

'I should think Miss Elwell would be even more severe.'

'I shouldn't,' said Philip. 'But I can see why you think so. She was very close to poor Uncle Ned, who died young. I don't really know much about him, though there's a photograph of him I was supposed to be rather like as a boy, and I hope I was. But I have my suspicions. Things have certainly been kept from me.'

25

4

'I must say I should like to see Philip married,' said Jane.

'There's time enough for that,' said Eliza. 'Look at all the rotten matches in the family! And we shouldn't see so much of him.'

'Perhaps,' said Jane. 'Anyway we oughtn't to think of that. But I should feel safer – he's so very much not the marrying sort.'

'Well, all sorts make a world.'

'You know, sometimes I've felt anxious – there have been tendencies in the family ...'

'We won't speak of them, Jane,' said Eliza firmly. 'And Philip shares lodgings with a clergyman. He's the most respectable of bachelors.'

'That *should* be all right,' said Jane grudgingly.

Philip was upstairs with George, who was having a bad day.

'Old boy, it felt like walking on raw stumps,' he said to Philip. 'You can't think what it's been like.'

'You've done quite right to stay up here,' said Philip. 'By the way, now we're on our own, there's something I've always wanted to ask you – what became of Uncle Ned?'

'Poor Ned!' said George. 'He was a delightful boy.'

'"Poor Ned",' echoed Philip. '"He was alive and is dead. There's no more to be said."'

'That's exactly the family line,' said George.

'He died before I was born, didn't he?'

'No, but you were a baby at the time.'

'I only know that he had a fruit farm, or something of the sort, with a friend in the Channel Islands. I gather something happened?'

'We don't quite know what, though perhaps Eliza does. She went over to clear things up. I've often wondered if there had been a suspicion of suicide. Eliza was like a clam. But she seems to have destroyed all his papers. No will turned up. But last time Ned was over here he told me he was leaving all he had to Eliza, because she wouldn't ever marry, as nothing on earth would induce her to leave your grandmother.'

'Perhaps he never made a will. I know only too well how people don't, for all their good intentions.'

'It could be. But if there was anything in the wording that might have hurt your grandmother, Eliza wouldn't have thought of herself for a moment.'

'She's rather magnificent.'

'You're rather like Ned,' said George. 'Your aunts are a bit concerned about it. You see, if I may put it delicately, he was so very much not a ladies' man.'

'Nor am I,' said Philip. 'I'm sure you knew that.'

'Of course,' said George. 'Mind you take your own way in life. I'm sure you'll never come to grief. All this sort of thing is very far away from me. I've been impotent for years, as I dare say your Aunt Jane has conveyed to you with her customary delicacy.'

'If she tried, she was too delicate for me,' said Philip.

'She doesn't mind, of course,' said George. 'Never did. I think she was rather pleased than otherwise. But she likes thinking she has been done out of something that was her due.'

'I expect she thinks *you* ought to mind.'

'How well you know her!'

'She's beginning to talk to me about "a man's life" – it seems she thinks I ought to be leading it.'

'I hope she's not really impertinent,' said George. 'Come to me if she is.'

'No, it's all very delicate,' said Philip. 'She says odd things about celibate clergy. Then she thinks James and I aren't properly grown up, living as we do like two undergraduates. She wonders if the Vicar likes it, and what people say. I don't think she really thinks evil. . . .'

'Pray God that keeps her quiet. If she thought evil she would say it. You can imagine. . . .'

'I'd rather not. I love her.'

'Yes,' said George. 'Some things ought never to be said, and are better not even imagined. If anyone says anything venomous to you, squeeze out the poison *at once*, as far as you can – but unforgivable things can't wholly be forgiven. One should never say them, whatever the temptation – and if one keeps them back they usually become unnecessary or out of date.'

'Aunt Eliza is more reserved.'

'Yes, good old Eliza,' said George. 'Eliza has often helped me out when there were things I wanted to hide from Jane. And how they nag at each other! Eliza is nearly always right, but I can't back her up all the time. After all, it's Jane who's my wife.'

'What a family you've married into, Uncle George!' said Philip. 'Is it because we're so inbred?'

'No, I expect it's like most others,' said George. 'Well, Jane is my wife, Eliza is – usually – my ally, though she doesn't like me much. Your mother was my friend. To begin with, she was the person Jane loved most in the world. Eliza was devoted to her too, but she cared most for your grandmother and your poor Uncle Ned. Fanny, your dear mother, rather liked to share you with Jane and me. She was so sorry for us for having no children of our own.'

'I loved coming to you. You spoiled me, of course.'

'We would have,' said George. 'But you had a strong nanny. And you were a nice child.'

'You both seemed so happy then.'

'We were, especially when we had you and your mother with us. I don't suppose you know yet the quite extraordinary happiness a young child in the house can give. You seem to get up every morning to a perfect day. But Jane and I were happy on the whole. We had married for love, at least I had.'

'Aunt Jane is still the most beautiful woman I know.'

'Perhaps you think so because she is so like your mother, but Jane had the finer features of the two.'

'And you and Aunt Jane had so much in common – far more than my mother could have had with Father.'

'Forgive me. I always found your father a bore, not good enough for Fanny. Yes, Jane and I loved hunting when we were much younger. Then we've always loved dogs, and Dart-i-moor and sketching....'

'I suppose I ought to go down,' said Philip some time after hearing the tea bell. 'I'll have your tea sent up to you.'

The aunts had a visitor; Miss Springfield had dropped in to tea.

'Philip here?' she asked.

'Upstairs,' said Jane. 'I don't know why he has to spend all these hours up there with George and that smelly old dog.'

'You're an ungrateful woman, Jane,' said Kate Springfield. 'I'm sure you wouldn't want to sit up there yourself.'

'As if I should dream of doing such a thing!'

'It's nice for George to have some companionship.'

'I hope he's not making too much use of poor Philip.'

'Nonsense,' said Eliza. 'Philip's fond of him, and they enjoy chatting together. Men do, you know.'

Eliza liked to assert herself, for Jane pretended that, as a spinster, she could know nothing about men. In fact Eliza had been far closer than Jane to their brothers, and had had plenty of opportunities for observing the marriages in the family — none of which seemed to have been made in heaven.

'I'm afraid George is filling him up with stories about the family,' said Jane. 'He was always inclined to be disloyal, and he knows Philip won't care.'

'Well, it will be all about people who are dead,' said Kate.

'They mightn't have liked to be gossiped about by George and Philip,' said Jane. 'And Philip will draw him out. And I don't think George is a good influence on him — he *will* encourage him with his drawing.'

'Naturally,' said Kate. 'Poor old George sacrificed his own talents, and he doesn't want Philip to do the same.'

'George could never had been a professional artist,' said Jane. 'He wouldn't have been good enough.'

'I'm not so sure of that,' said Kate. 'But Philip could be. Here he is — Filippo!'

'Donna Caterina! How's Lassie?'

'How angry he'd be to hear you call him that. He's gone back to being Musso. It's time we buried that hatchet.'

'You're not going back to Italy?' asked Jane disapprovingly.

'As soon as possible after Christmas,' said Kate. 'It's quite safe, you know. Always was. The finishing schools have already gone back. The Italians are very forgiving.'

'Forgiving!' exclaimed Jane. 'It's for us to do the forgiving.'

'What have they done to us?' asked Philip. 'What have we to forgive?'

'I'm not thinking of ourselves,' said Jane. 'I'm thinking of the poor Abyssinians.'

'Then it's for them to forgive,' said Philip. 'I do hate our newspapers. It seems to me an impertinence to either side for us to forgive what they have done to each other – or to refuse to forgive. And, as Christians, if there *were* anything for us to forgive, we are bound to forgive it.'

'Bravo Filippo!' said Kate.

'There's such a thing as justice,' said Jane, tossing her head.

'*Is* there?' said Philip.

'Well, I'm going back thankfully some time in January,' said Kate. 'You should come, Philip, and do a bit of art study.'

'Philip has better things to do,' said Eliza.

'Making wills, and drawing up contracts and marriage settlements,' said Philip bitterly. 'Pacifying people who want to sue their neighbours, or writing stiff letters for them.'

'The real work of the world,' said Eliza. 'You can't expect it always to be amusing.'

'A pity to waste yourself on it if you're good for better things,' said Kate. 'Why not give yourself at least six months' holiday or what they call a "sabbatical year"? After all, you're your own boss, I imagine.'

'He'd get out of touch,' said Jane quickly. This was a regular remark in the family if anyone wanted to go anywhere.

'Ridiculous woman,' she said, after Miss Springfield had gone.

'I don't know,' said Philip. 'I envy her with all my heart.'

'Laying down the law like that,' said Eliza – another regular remark in the family. Had Kate advocated a course of action that was approved, such as matrimony or sticking to the law, such an impertinence would have been called 'taking an interest'.

'Well, one day I shall break away,' said Philip. 'I can't stick in that office all my life.'

'Can't you do your drawing in your spare time?' said Eliza.

'Not really enough. I ought to make it my full-time work. The people I admire are those who enjoy their whole lives, and make every bit of them interesting – not just their spare time, when they're generally tired.'

'I admire people who stick to their jobs,' said Jane relentlessly.

'I'm sorry for them, if they have to and they don't like it,' said Philip. 'But anyone can stick to a job if he must. I admire people who have the courage to break free and do what they like.'

'It doesn't need any courage to do what one likes,' said Jane.

'On the contrary, I think it often needs great courage,' said Philip. 'Think how few people do it! Of course there aren't many people who really like anything – I never thought of that.'

'James Freeling can't think like that,' said Jane. 'Yet he must have a lot of dreary chores to do – he can't always be in a green vestment.'

'He might stop doing them.'

'I don't care for clergymen who give up,' said Eliza. 'It never looks well.'

'James wouldn't do that,' said Philip. 'But there are different sorts of clergymen, you know. He might give up pastoral work and be a scholar or a schoolmaster, or a chaplain somewhere. He's begun a thesis, and in his present life he never has the time to get on with it.'

'One thing he couldn't be is a minor canon,' said Eliza with a smile. 'He has no ear. It would be painful to hear him sing the service.'

'Yes, indeed, poor dear.'

'And I think you said he's not much of a preacher?' said Jane.

'So you see he's chiefly useful at St Simon's for pastoral work, which he detests,' said Philip. 'He would do much better in some other sort of clerical job.'

'But you'd miss him if he moved.'

'Unless I moved too. He might go somewhere where I could join him. If he took a chaplaincy abroad, for example.'

'Philip!'

31

'Well, why not? I can do my drawing anywhere where I have peace.'

'It's not as if you were married to Mr Freeling. You don't have to go where he goes.'

'I'm even less wedded to my work at the office. Let's leave things alone till we see how they work out. I could be the first one to go. I'm more footloose than James because I have all the world before me to choose from. His choice would have to be more limited, as he is a priest.'

'If women try to make you work, you should make them weep,' said James, when Philip reported this talk to him. 'It's their share of the human predicament according to the poet — if you can call that man a poet.'

'I should have to die to draw tears from Aunt Eliza,' said Philip.

5

'Philip, it's time you began to think of getting married,' said Jane.

'Don't pester the poor boy,' said Eliza. 'He's got plenty of time before him.'

'I don't know about that,' said Jane in a sinister voice.

'Let's leave it alone,' said Philip.

'Other people don't,' said Jane, angrily shaking a piece of paper.

'Jane, I begged you not to mention it to Philip,' said Eliza.

'He must take some responsibility for it.'

'What on earth is it?'

'Your Aunt Jane has had this filthy anonymous letter,' said Eliza. 'I told her she ought to get rid of it at once and think no more of it. I should be ashamed to pay any attention to anything anonymous.'

'I don't want it to happen again,' said Jane. 'You must see that it doesn't.'

'You'd better let me look at it,' said Philip. 'If I can find out who it comes from, there won't be any more.'

'Poor Philip, he'll be so distressed,' said Eliza.

'Oh, please show it me!' said Philip. 'Or I shall imagine something worse.'

'I don't see how it could be much worse,' said Jane.

'Hm,' said Philip reading it. 'It's only a vague attack on my morals, and some rude words.'

'It shows what some people think about you,' said Jane.

'It only shows what one beast is prepared to say,' said Eliza. 'And without daring to put his name to it.'

'You take it very calmly,' said Jane.

'The only way to take it,' said Philip. 'I'm a lawyer,

remember. Now, who can have sent you this filthy rubbish, and why? Have we any enemies?'

'I suppose you and Mr Dolmidge must have made some,' said Eliza.

'It's always a risk in our profession,' said Philip. 'But why write to Aunt Jane?'

'Because they know she's the only one of us who would talk about it, ' said Eliza nastily. 'The rest of us would just tear it up and despise it.'

'If you do talk about it, Aunt Jane, be careful to say that you've consulted your solicitor. If that gets back to the brute, it may frighten him. Libel is a very serious offence.'

'Who could it have been?'

'I don't know,' said Philip. 'Of course there's that new man, Bayne, trying to take over some of our work.'

'Depend upon it, it's him,' said Eliza. 'Trying to hurt you and your practice.'

'Very likely,' said Philip, seeking a distraction. 'Aunt Jane, don't you remember that Welsh solicitor who asked his rival to tea and tried to poison him?'

'In the buttered scones!' said Jane. 'He said "Excuse fingers" and gave the poor man a scone full of arsenic.'

'How we loved that case!' said Philip. 'You had a bet on with Father that Armstrong would get off – and we really hoped he would, though it turned out that he'd poisoned his wife and several other people.'

'Yes, I used to send you the news when you were at school,' said Jane. 'He had a splendid counsel, and it was a lovely trial.'

'And the headmaster's wife – silly woman – said, "Couldn't you find something nicer to occupy your mind?" She complained that Armstrong had told a pack of lies. Well, wouldn't she, to save her neck?'

'But there was one very pathetic thing,' said Jane. 'His children ran out to buy an evening paper on the day of the verdict, and the kind newsagent pretended to be sold out.'

'I remember,' said Philip. 'It made me cry.'

'Armstrong wouldn't let them come to see him in prison,' said Jane. 'He didn't want to leave them with that memory. He can't have been all bad.'

'Perhaps Bayne isn't,' said Philip easily. 'But I won't go to tea with him for all that.'

'If you'd get married, it would be the end of all this nonsense,' said Jane.

'Not necessarily. Bayne won't have your touching faith in marriage as a steadier for a man. After all, he's a lawyer of a sort and knows too much about it. Seriously, it's not worth another thought. If you've any more letters like that, just keep them for me. It will help me to find out who my well-wisher is.'

Jane was always easier and cosier when Eliza was not there.

'You know, darling,' she said, 'sometimes I think your uncle and I made a great mistake to join forces with your Aunt Eliza when your grandmother died. We were happier before.'

'You were both younger and in better health,' said Philip.

'And your dear mother was alive. She had a much nicer character than your Aunt Eliza. Your aunt is so hard. Of course your uncle is getting old, but she doesn't make allowances if he's a bit messy. Your mother would have, she was always his friend. I still miss her, and always shall as long as I live.'

'I was lucky not to have a stepmother,' said Philip. 'With you and Aunt Eliza there I never missed a mother, but she left a gap dangerously open.'

'I know – like those two poor Faringdon boys, with that horrible German woman,' said Jane. 'Well, just before you were born I went with your mother to make her will. She wanted to tie up her money on her children in case she died and your father married again. "Gilbert might marry anyone," she said. I told your grandmother, who said in her dry way: "What a lot of fuss! It isn't every woman who'd marry Gilbert." I said: "It's enough if there's one, and she's a wrong one."'

'I always wondered why she married him.'

'Oh, Gilbert was very good-looking at one time,' said Jane. 'And he wasn't such a stick when she was alive. He dried up afterwards, poor man. Your mother was quite right to take precautions. She knew he had nearly married a dreadful woman before he met her.'

'What happened? How did he escape?'

'Oh, luckily she had a scandal,' said Jane ruthlessly. 'Your

35

Aunt Eliza would be horrified to hear us talk like this. She's very loyal to our generation, and anyway she'd think you ought to honour your father, much as she disliked him.'

'Did she? I shouldn't have thought he was positive enough to be dislikeable.'

'Well, your grandmother loathed him. And anyway it's so natural to dislike in-laws. One never thinks them good enough for the family – and usually they aren't.'

'There you are, you see!' said Philip. 'I'd better not marry. You'd adore my children, if I had any, and hate my wife. They'd be family, she'd only be an in-law.'

'I'm afraid you may be right,' said Jane laughing. 'Unfortunately I can't think of a distant cousin for you.'

'I know how you all hate Cousin Rosa – that arch in-law.'

'She's a bad lot,' said Jane.

'That's rather much to say, isn't it?' said Philip. 'I know she's false and sanctimonious and rather bossy – horrid woman.'

'My dear, you don't know everything.'

'So I gathered,' said Philip. 'Aunt Eliza once told me she hadn't been good to Cousin Bertie, which rather surprised me. She has always made so much of her "big happy family".'

'Just like your Aunt Eliza!' said Jane, provoked. 'Didn't she once tell you that poor Winnie died from an escape of gas? Of course the wretched woman gassed herself. So inconsiderate – really dangerous for other people.'

'Well, what's specially wrong with Cousin Rose?'

'Adultery, just that,' said Jane trenchantly. 'She had a child by another man. We all hoped Bertie would get rid of her, as he could have by our laws, but he took her back. Then there were more children.'

'And then it would have been too late,' said Philip. 'Which of them was it?'

'The illegit? Fortunately it died.'

'Who was the father?'

'I've forgotten. But to do her justice, he was a gentleman. She didn't go off with a hairdresser or a chauffeur.'

'You astonish me. You make me think of one of Chesterton's stories: "Where would you hide a pebble? On the beach."'

'What do you mean, darling?'

'The last place you'd look for a love-child would be in a "big, happy family". One can't imagine how Cousin Rosa had the time for it – philoprogenitive as she has always been.'

'Like the cat she is!' said Jane. 'But there was no need to hide the poor little bastard except in the grave.'

'We can't call it a "bastard", you know. She was still married to Cousin Bertie, so he was its legal father.'

'Poor brute!' said Jane. 'But he had only himself to thank for that.'

'You were rather a long time with your aunts today,' said James. 'Is anything wrong?'

'Not really. Aunt Jane was rather upset at getting a dirty anonymous letter. You may as well read it.'

'Hum,' said James. 'Not very nice. I hope you soothed her down?'

'Yes,' said Philip. 'One must just hope there aren't any more. Have you heard about people getting any?'

'If you're asking delicately if I've had one myself, the answer is "No",' said James, smiling. 'It's a thing the clergy often get, I believe. Especially celibates.'

'Aunt Jane says the celibacy of the clergy is "unnatural".'

'Well, the "natural man" is rather a scamp, isn't he?' said James. 'Of course you couldn't tell her that our life is supernatural.'

'Of course not,' said Philip. 'One can't talk religion to one's family.'

'Except in times of bereavement.'

'Then, of course. But Aunt Eliza is more reasonable, being happily celibate herself and Higher Church – or does one say "more High Church" or "High Churcher"?'

'Not the last, I should think. One says "more Cartholic",' said James demurely.

'She said she'd never go for confession to a married priest – not that I think she has ever gone to anyone, or that she could have anything to say that could interest the most inquisitive clergyman's wife.'

'That alone might be something she wouldn't want to come out,' said James, smiling.

'But seriously, it's disagreeable to have an anonymous

letter-writer about,' said Philip. 'One of the nastiest sort of vermin. This may be a single blow, but she may strike again.'

'She?'

'Well, they often are female – like poisoners.'

'I suppose she might write to the Vicar,' said James. 'Would he be enough of a gentleman to ignore it?'

'Well, you see, Aunt Jane wasn't enough of a lady, but Aunt Eliza would have been.'

'If the Vicar tackles me about it, I shall resign,' said James.

'Don't do that. Say you'll consult your solicitor.'

'And what will my solicitor advise?'

'Do nothing whatever. When and if we want to make a move, let's do it when we please. One mustn't be stampeded by vermin.'

'"Stampeded by vermin." Picturesque phrase!'

'Yes,' said Philip, laughing. 'It sounds like Hamelin or Bishop Hatto.'

'But could you ever really uproot yourself?'

'I suppose you have a Bible, James. Chuck it over.'

James handed him the volume, and Philip turned over the leaves.

'My text is taken from the first chapter of the Book of Ruth,' said Philip. 'Part of the sixteenth verse. "Intreat me not to leave thee, or to return from following after thee: for whither thou goest, I will go; and where thou lodgest, I will lodge."'

'Could you really pull out of the place, and the firm and your family?'

'I'd have to come back to see them every year. But the uprooting might do me a lot of good.'

'It might do you good to be a bit detached from me,' said James. 'You might make new friends – you might even marry.'

'Don't talk like the aunts!' said Philip. 'It doesn't suit you. And would you like it?'

'I should hate it,' said James.

Philip kissed him on the forehead. 'Then talk sense,' he said.

'Seriously, I do sometimes fear your feeling frustrated, living with someone like me,' said James.

'Dearest, your service is perfect freedom. I seem to be talking the language of your trade today.'

'I won't retort on you with torts,' said James. 'And, talking of torts, I wonder who the nasty creature is who wrote that letter?'

'Aunt Eliza suggested it was a business rival, and I pretended to think so too, to quiet the aunts,' said Philip. 'But I've no idea. In books it would be some wretched woman with a blighted affection for me.'

'But you can't think of one?'

'I shouldn't notice that sort of thing,' said Philip. 'There may be lots.'

6

'Your auntie has just rung up to ask if you were back,' said Miss Snape.

'Which one, Miss Snape?' asked Philip. 'Did she leave a message?'

'It was Mrs Keyworth – such a sweet lady. She just asked, very nicely, if you would ring her back after lunch.'

'Then it's nothing urgent,' said Philip with relief, imagining that his aunts would not want the service of their own luncheon by a newish parlourmaid to be interrupted.

'Such a bore!' exclaimed Jane, when he telephoned. 'Your uncle's niece, Mary Keyworth, has invited herself over to luncheon on Thursday. One couldn't well refuse to let her come.'

'Hardly.'

'What does she want to come now for?' asked Jane impatiently. 'She never has before.'

'I don't know. She's Norman Keyworth's daughter, isn't she?'

'No, Stanley's. She's a woman doctor, if you please!'

'Indeed?'

'I wondered if you could possibly come too? I know you sometimes take Thursday afternoon off. Your Aunt Eliza and I would like to have your support.'

'I'll try. I'll ring you up this evening.'

'I suppose your aunts will want to marry you to this Dr Mary Keyworth,' said James. 'They seem to want to marry you off.'

'They do, but they don't like Uncle George's family. He's never been allowed to have one of them in the house before, that I remember. Mary seems to have invited herself.'

'What's wrong with them?'

'I've never much taken to them myself, the little I've seen of them. But that's personal and indefinable. My aunts think the family is not good enough for us – not that we're anything to boast of.'

'Oh, your firm is old and more than respectable,' said James. 'I don't know anything about your mother's people.'

'The Elwells like to call themselves "landed gentry", and perhaps they still are, but it's in another county. Grandma's family, the Shrubsoles, counted for more as they lived near, and she ruled the roost as a matriarch. But their place was sold years ago, so they're lucky if they're counted as "gentry" still.'

'Well, our place was sold too.'

'Yes, but you are in the Book of Life. Sir Walter Elliot could find you there when he picked it up for "occupation in an idle hour, and consolation in a distressed one". If enough people died you'd be "the Reverend Sir James".'

'I hope they won't,' said James. 'Quite apart from my natural affection for my brother and his children, a baronet-priest doesn't sound right to me.'

'Oh, I think it's rather nice, and old-fashioned and High Church,' said Philip.

'It's rather a silly title, neither one thing nor the other,' said James. 'A baronet seems destined to be found dead in a library, as in detective novels. It's all right for Father to be Sir Michael, because his patients think it's a medical distinction, and he can charge them more.'

Mary Keyworth turned out to be a tall young woman of about Philip's age – so discreet in voice, manner and appearance that he suspected it was contrived for his aunts' benefit. 'A bit too good to be true,' one of them was sure to say (probably Jane), while the other would take up her defence. Philip determined on neutrality while he waited to see his uncle's reaction.

'Dr Keyworth?' he said.

'Nonsense, Philip, I'm Mary,' she said. 'Don't you remember children's parties at my grandmother's?'

'Uncle George's mother' had been a beloved figure in Philip's childhood. She had even asked to be called 'Granny Keyworth'.

41

'Oh yes,' said Philip. 'You used to cheat at snakes and ladders.'

'No, I never!' said Mary. 'You were such a prim little boy I was rather afraid of you. I'd been told to be kind to you because you had no mother.'

'The silly things people tell children! How I should have resented it! I'm sure that wasn't Granny Keyworth.'

'No, it was my fool of a governess,' said Mary. 'Anyway I learned young that it wasn't my vocation to deal with children.'

'What is your line?'

'Well, older people,' said Mary, looking cautiously round. Then, like so many people with specialized interests, she abandoned caution and talked fluently about her work and her ambitions for it. Everyone listened with well-bred patience, though Jane fiddled with the mustard-pot.

'You see,' Mary explained, 'I came over to stay for a day or two at Uncle Norman's, and it seemed a chance to come and see you all, and to find how Uncle George was keeping.'

'Norman has become very much the country gentleman, I hear,' said Jane, far from admiringly. 'I'm told he's got quite a big place at Madingfold.'

'Oh yes,' said Mary. 'It's all very nice. But he was anxious that I should come and take a look at Uncle George. We seldom hear anything of him.'

'I wish you could persuade him to change his doctor,' said Jane.

'No, I'm too old for changes and I hate them,' said George. 'I shall stick to good old Henville-Poke. He's probably as much use to me as anyone else.'

'He's rather an old woman,' said Eliza.

'Well, so are we,' said Jane.

'And I hope to live to be one,' said Mary, laughing. 'But I'll give up practice before that. Henville-Poke has got a bit behind the times.'

This started off the Ancient and Modern argument, always a favourite theme in that house.

'People are far too anxious to be modern,' said Jane.

'Do you like modern art, Mary?' said Eliza. 'It seems to me so childish.'

'That's a big question, Miss Elwell. I like some

42

contemporary painters very much, and others not at all. I dare say in every age there has been a great deal of bad painting.'

'I don't see signs of much good in this,' said George. 'Hardly anyone can draw nowadays, except Philip.'

'Different ages are good at different things,' said Mary. 'Or at the same things in a different way. The years since the war have been a great age for literature, and no good at all for music – at least in my opinion.'

'But so many books nowadays are nasty,' said Eliza. 'You can hardly take a book from the library and not find something beastly, and unnecessary, in it.'

'You could say the same of Shakespeare,' said Philip.

The talk was now well under way. Shakespeare was Shakespeare – "others abide our question". But so much in his age was too coarse for our refined taste; and now there seemed to be a reaction towards coarseness. Certainly our age was not one in which nice manners flourished. Most modern young people were odious. Possibly they were more natural? Perhaps they had a happier relationship with their parents? One hardly knew.

'Progress' was such a deceptive word. In the arts it only occurred in a zigzag sort of way, as it was usually a question of technical advance (thus Philip).

There had been no music greater than that of Bach (Mary).

No painter greater than Piero (Philip).

No poet greater than Shakespeare (lip-service patriotically rendered by Jane and Eliza, in spite of all his 'unnecessary beastliness').

But in the sciences, where technical advance was nearly everything, there had been progress. Dentistry, for example.

'And thank heaven for that!' said Eliza.

'Also more generally in medical science,' said Mary. 'Uncle George, will you please let me look you over thoroughly after lunch? I feel sure we can help you. You don't mind, Aunt Jane?'

'Oh no. I only hope you can persuade your uncle to take better care of himself.'

'I wonder why she came,' said Jane, when Mary had gone

43

upstairs with George. 'She *said* Norman wanted to know how he was. At any rate it's better than if he came himself.'

'It's nice of him to want to know how his brother is,' said Eliza.

'It's the least he can do,' said Jane, tossing her head. 'It's his duty.'

'It's also the most he can do,' said Philip. 'Uncle George wouldn't at all like him to do more. And have you never thought how unimaginably better the world would be if everyone did his duty, even if no one did a thing more?'

'I don't know about that,' said Eliza. 'Think of what people do for charity.'

'Most of it wouldn't be needed, if everyone did his duty,' said Philip.

'Anyway, Mary seems quite a nice young woman,' said Eliza. 'Not too modern. She doesn't smoke or have her hair cut short.'

'Rather too inclined to lay down the law,' said Jane.

'After all, she's a doctor,' said Philip. 'She's used to giving orders.'

'Very unfeminine,' said Jane. 'I don't know what her father thinks. I would never go to a woman doctor, I'd have no confidence.'

'I think I should rather like it,' said Eliza. 'When Allchin retires I think quite seriously of going to Mrs Plumley. Kate swears by her.'

'Anyhow, I hope Mary manages to suppress that frightful portable Turkish bath thing,' said Jane. 'I'm always terrified that George will electrocute himself, or blow himself up, or boil himself alive in it.'

'I hear her coming downstairs. But I suppose it would be only natural for us to be talking about her,' said Philip. 'Well, Mary, what is your report on your patient?'

'I think he rather lets himself go, if you see what I mean,' said Mary. 'If I might, I should like to recommend some stiff massage. Do you think he'd agree, Aunt Jane?'

'I wouldn't be too hopeful,' said Jane. 'He hates every effort or anything new.'

'We can but try,' said Eliza. 'After all, he's a sensible man, and he ought to welcome anything that will do him good.'

'But will he believe that massage will do him good?' said Jane.

'"Ay, there's the rub,"' said Philip. 'Oh, forgive the horrible pun!'

Mary gave Philip a lift into the town in her car. 'We'll have to form some sort of alliance, if you see what I mean,' she told him. 'You must work on Aunt Jane, and on Uncle George if he gives you the chance. I'll look out for the right masseur – or masseuse – and make another visit and try to impose him.'

'But you won't be long at Madingfold?' said Philip, not unhopefully. He was afraid she was inclined to order him about.

'Not this time,' she said. 'But I can come for a weekend whenever I like. I suppose you wouldn't come over?'

'I'd rather not,' said Philip. 'I hardly know them.'

'And Aunt Jane wouldn't like it,' added Mary sarcastically.

'No, she wouldn't,' said Philip with a smile.

'You *do* let her dictate to you!' said Mary.

'Well, it's policy not to offend her,' said Philip, who had no wish to go to Madingfold. 'If we do, then goodbye to our plan. If you want a neutral meeting-place, perhaps you wouldn't mind coming to see James and me any time you are near.'

George remained upstairs, but Kate Springfield had dropped in to tea.

'How did the visit go off?' she asked.

'Not too badly,' said Eliza. 'Mary is quite a nice girl, quiet and with good manners. And we got Philip to come and help us.'

'How did Philip take to her?'

'That's hardly the point,' said Jane coldly. 'Mary came to have a look at her uncle. The Norman Keyworths seemed to think it was time they asked after him.'

'And George reacted favourably?'

'I think so, on the whole, though I don't know how he'll like her recommendation to him of having massage.'

'Do him all the good in the world,' said Kate. 'And how did Philip react?' she added irrepressibly. 'Usually he hates girls.'

45

'I thought he quite liked her,' said Eliza. 'She drove him home afterwards.'

'He was polite, of course,' said Jane more coldly. 'I don't know that he particularly liked her.'

'You don't think he's likely to be specially interested in her?'

'I hope not,' said Jane.

'Why not?'

'We don't want another marriage with that family,' said Jane. 'George was the only one possible among them.'

'The old lady was all right,' said Kate. 'She was a Colquhoun, wasn't she?'

'But the old man was impossible,' said Jane. 'I remember a family Christmas dinner, and he cut the plum pudding with a steel knife!'

'They've come on a bit since then,' said Kate. 'Norman is quite the squire at Madingfold, so I hear.'

'And I suppose we've come down in the world,' said Jane. 'Now the place is sold, and no one remembers Grandpa.'

'But I still think Philip could do better for himself,' said Eliza.

'I quite agree,' said Jane. 'But is it likely? He hates going out, so he's not likely to meet many girls. Mary is clever, that's an attraction, or I suppose it would be to some people.'

'But she's a doctor. She hasn't got time for family life.'

'I dare say she'd give it up quite cheerfully if she had a chance of marrying well,' said Jane.

'She'd be a fool if she did,' said Kate. 'There's a great future for women in medicine. Look at Dr Plumley!'

'I rather agree,' said Eliza. 'Mary impresses me as serious.'

'All the better if Philip doesn't marry,' said Kate. 'He can give himself up to his art. My dear Jane, you'd like to take them away from what they really want to do, and settle them down to a humdrum marriage, when they don't care a button for each other.'

'The world has to go on,' said Jane.

'I can't think why it need,' said Kate. 'None of us here has helped it along, and it's no business of ours. One should encourage people to do what they like.'

'You talk like Philip,' said Jane. 'And if you believe in people doing what they like, why don't you go and live in

Italy? You're always running down the English climate.'

'I'm too old and set in my ways,' said Kate. 'I ought to have done it years ago, that was my mistake. When I was young enough I hadn't the courage to do what I really liked.'

7

Philip, arriving one Sunday when his aunts were not yet back from their respective places of worship, found George sitting in the dining-room. His false teeth lay on the table.

'The dratted things flew out like a covey of partridges,' said George.

'I should leave them out till you need them,' said Philip.

'I dursn't!' said George. 'Your Aunt Jane would think it as bad as being without trousers.' But he let them lie.

'Had a bad week?' asked Philip sympathetically.

'Not too good. Do you know, if things go on like this I think I shall ask Henville-Poke what he thinks about massage.'

'A very sound idea,' said Philip, relieved of his responsibility to forward it.

'My niece Mary is all for it,' said George. 'I'm quite surprised that didn't set your Aunt Jane dead against it.'

Philip laughed.

'You may laugh,' said George. 'But she can't endure my family. Agreed, she couldn't be expected to take to my brothers – "they never went to good schools".'

'But Uncle George!' said Philip, now laughing heartily. Then he pulled himself together. 'Why didn't they? You went to Charterhouse.'

'And had my life bullied out of me. So Mother took pity on the boys and had them educated privately. It never occurred to her that they would probably have been among the bullies.'

'So perhaps it was better so,' said Philip.

'No, I think some of their corners would have been rubbed off,' said George. 'I don't altogether blame Jane for never asking them here. Anyway, I don't really want them.'

'Surely they used to come?' said Philip. 'I vaguely remember

Uncle Norman and Aunt Winnie – as I was supposed to call them – coming over to a croquet party, and a boy called Derek.'

'You must have been very small then. It was ages ago, and in your grandmother's time. Poor Winnie gassed herself – out of boredom, I fancy.'

'What became of Derek?'

'He's in his father's business now. He turned out much better than I expected, and he's quite a good chap,' said George. 'He was a ghastly youngster, always blackmailing poor old Norman. "Give me this, give me that, or I'll do what Mother did, and you drove her to".'

'Nice!' said Philip.

'But of course Norman didn't give in. He just told Derek to get on with it.'

'George, your disgusting teeth on the table!' exclaimed Jane, entering in the bad temper that so often follows church-going.

'Just having a little rest, my dear,' said George.

'I don't know that you ever do anything else,' said Jane. 'Put them in, I can't bear to look at you. You've been mumbling away to Philip. Of course he pretends to understand you. He spoils you, and you're very bad for him, the worst possible example. He's becoming as shabbily dressed as you. At one time a professional man wouldn't dare to go out on Sundays as badly turned out as he is. It can't do his practice much good. He probably went to church like that too.'

'But there I wore a cassock over it,' said Philip.

'And *that* probably did your practice no good either. But that's no business of mine, thank goodness. But I will not have my husband looking like an old tramp. People will be giving you pennies. I dare say it's happened already. You're a perfect disgrace to us. You may not care what you look like, but it's we who will be blamed for it. I don't know what Eliza will say....'

During this tirade Eliza came in. 'Oh, that's enough, Jane,' she said. 'It's Sunday. Let poor George have a rest. After all, he's not going out.'

'You never back me up!' said Jane angrily. 'You know you agree with everything I've said. You've said it time and time again yourself. I couldn't expect any support from Philip, of course. He's rapidly becoming as bad as George himself. But for you to go against me!'

'I shall go and take off my hat,' said Eliza finally.

After luncheon, which had been eaten in a silent but threatening gloom, the Keyworths retired to their rooms, and Philip was left with Eliza.

'I sometimes wonder how I can go on living with your Aunt Jane,' said Eliza. 'She does nag so. Then I have to defend your poor uncle – and of course he's getting old and some of his little ways are trying. Your mother had a much nicer character than your aunt.'

She then began to wonder what sort of an account Mary would have taken back to Madingfold. Things had been all very well (perhaps) when George had gone up to London every day, and until a few years ago he still had his mother's to go to when he wanted a change. Meanwhile the house had been almost entirely run for the two sisters. Now he had retired, a bit more ought to be done for him. First of all this room, the morning-room, might be made over to him; it would be far better to have him on the ground floor so that he didn't have to struggle up and down the stairs. Besides, the gentlemen's lavatory was downstairs and Jane hated him to use the other one.

'And I don't much care for it myself,' said Eliza honestly. 'But it would be cruel to make him hobble upstairs and downstairs.'

'Then you could turn his present bedroom into the morning-room,' said Philip. 'It's exactly above this.'

Eliza thought that would do very well. If George were settled downstairs it would be far easier for the maids to bring him trays when he was unwell; and the old dog could have his basket outside his door in the hall, better than up on the landing, for one wouldn't hear him if he barked.

'But your Aunt Jane will never agree.'

'One would have to make her think it was her own idea,' said Philip. 'It would be fatal if she thought it was done to make a good impression at Madingfold.'

'I should think so!' said Eliza loyally. 'As if we cared what Norman thought!'

'Philip not staying to tea?' asked Jane, when she came down.

'No, he said he had to get back. Mary had rung up to say she might drop in on them.'

'They seem to have got very thick,' said Jane with a snort.

'Oh, I think it was just to talk over a possible masseuse for George.'

'Where was Mary coming from? Madingfold?'

'I don't know. I didn't ask.'

'I don't trust her, I think she's sneaky,' said Jane. 'I fancy she's out to make trouble.'

'What on earth can she do?'

'We'll know when she's done it and it's too late. Of course she can get anything out of Philip – he's too simple and straightforward himself. Sometimes I'm afraid he must be a rotten lawyer.'

'You know Philip wouldn't say anything about us that we wouldn't like.'

'Not on purpose,' said Jane. 'But Mary would do the cross-questioning. She could make him say what she liked – and if he didn't, she could twist what he said into what she wanted him to say.'

'I don't think there's any danger of that,' said Eliza.

Philip went out sadly. He was leaving three out of the four people whom he loved most in the world, and they did not love each other. Surely there must once have been love between them: George and Jane had married, and presumably for love; and they must have had one a brotherly, the other a sisterly affection for Eliza. Could such a feeling completely die, or was it just numbed? At the moment he felt most pity for brave old Eliza. So upright, so patient. It would infuriate the two sufferers if they knew, George so arthritic, Jane so 'highly strung' – while Eliza was 'as strong as a horse'.

His memories went back to earlier scenes. Once, when he was a very small boy, his parents had left him to stay with Eliza and his grandmother. He had had a little bed in Eliza's long room: he did not know how much he remembered from that time, or from having seen it again. There was a wall almost covered with wedding groups and other family photographs: his mother as a bride was attended by two little cousins (out of Cousin Rosa's brood), and two rather too mature sisters of his father's in big, very ugly hats. All these photographs were growing dim, and so, he thought, were all the passions that had lain behind them. On another wall was a large reproduction of the Sistine Madonna, and the heads of Beatrice Cenci and Lady Hamilton.

In his mind's eye he suddenly saw a green and white plate on which Eliza had brought him an exquisite peach from the garden, and it seemed the symbol of all those days.

Some of the tenderest youthful memories are bound to be connected with things to eat. He saw Jane, when he visited her and George in the little house where they lived before Grandma's death, giving him a large ripe plum, purple on the outside and gold within. He loved that little house whose garden ended in a stream. This Jane peopled for him with elves, which were not always beneficent beings, for her imagination always had an astringent dash of cruelty. Later, when he was at the kindergarten, she invented a world of German spies for him. When he was a schoolboy and the war was over they were replaced by poisoners. Poison cases, after all, were the 'nicest' murders; there were the thickest motives, the most numerous suspects, and nothing 'unnecessary' or 'beastly' – no sex, at least not on the surface. Besides, she herself had come near to one; once she had stayed at the same hotel as a sister of the unfortunate Mrs Greenwood. Was her husband guilty (for certainly she had been poisoned)? Had his daughter saved his neck by perjury, swearing that she had drunk from the same claret-jug as her mother? This raised a fascinating problem: would you have done what she (perhaps) did, or wouldn't you? They endlessly debated it.

George had been the most fascinating uncle, producing lovely and original toys that he had made in his spare time. Somewhere in a cupboard there was still the beautiful eagle kite that flapped its wings and terrified small birds when they flew it.

Philip's childhood had not been unclouded, in spite of all this love and happiness. There had been a forbidding father, and the trials of school. If he remembered it better than any other period of his life, it was because he most often thought

52

of it. Thought of any continuous period after adolescence must bring memories of sins and gaffes; shamefully it was the latter for which one blushed more deeply. How could anyone write an honest autobiography, or wish for the publication of his diaries or letters?

The three in that household had always loved him, and they still did. He had never been an object of contention between them. If Jane were sometimes impatient of his affection for George, it was not out of jealousy; she just thought he was giving George undeserved support. They had never tried to be parents to him; they had cared too much for his mother to wish to take her place, and so little for his father (though they believed themselves to admire him) that his place did not seem to them worth filling. But if, happily, Philip had not been a bone of contention, unhappily he had in no way been a bond between them. Yet perhaps, indirectly, he might have been of use. He kept their affections alive as they were turned on him; he might be the peach or the plum, as it were, the thing that made their torpid juices flow.

He felt sad, and the late afternoon was chilly. A dreary hymn ran in his head:

> By many deeds of shame
> We learn that love grows cold.

He had never quite known what it meant, but it must be something utterly depressing. What had happened to them might happen to him and James. They might go on living together from habit, with ever cooling affection. He might begin to nag – for he was so like Jane. There was not anyone, not even a dog, to hold them together.

Then the watery autumnal sun sent a pale beam that fell upon one of the gorse bushes on the heath, which was still in flower. There are always flowers somewhere on them, however few. These were lit up, bright and golden.

Philip felt a great consolation, timeless and without conscious thought. Burdens dropped off him, his own cares and the cares of others; he felt that underneath all was well. Then, as thought reasserted itself, he wondered at his sudden happiness; it was not useful to rationalize it, but perhaps he owed it to the flash of gold among the surrounding greyness, the sign of life in a decaying world. 'The world is very evil,' another hymn proclaimed: just now it threatened to become infinitely more evil than it had ever been before, if the gathering war-clouds broke. James and he so dreaded and hated the idea of war that they never spoke of it, though each saw the pain in the other's face on a day of particularly acute crisis. But in this moment of happiness he felt: *There lives the dearest freshness deep down things.* Stupid and ungrateful people would speak of 'wishful thinking'. At any rate it was more useful than 'fearful thinking' – a dash of it from time to time helped one to live.

8

Philip, happily delayed by the flowers, arrived to find James and Mary already at tea: they seemed quite comfortable together.

'We didn't wait,' said James. 'Doctors are always busy, and I was sure Dr Keyworth had to go on somewhere.'

'And Father Freeling has evensong or something,' said Mary. 'But he insisted on saving the last crumpet for you.'

'Precious, like Sappho's apple – it *was* Sappho's, wasn't it? – at the end of the topmost bough,' said Philip. 'Or St Crumpet, like Ruskin.'

'Well, it must be the most buttery,' said James practically. 'Though I don't know that Ruskin was.'

Miss Snape came in with fresh tea. 'Now it was very naughty of you not to ring,' she said archly. 'Was poor Mr Milsom to drink stewed tea?'

'I didn't want to bring you upstairs again,' said Philip. 'I knew Doris must be out.'

'I'm not like these modern girls,' said Miss Snape. 'I never mind work. Not like that Doris – and though it's Sunday afternoon I doubt if she sees so much as the outside of a church.'

'You've met Dr Keyworth, I suppose?'

'Yes, Father James introduced us. You have a very sweet auntie, Doctor.'

If Mary made a face, it fortunately went unnoticed.

'"Father James",' she murmured. 'But you're not "Mr Philip"?'

'No, not yet, but I shall be if she talks to the "aunties" much more. And you may become "Doctor Mary". But I'm not sure if you ought to say "Father James". Are you High enough Church or High Church enough?'

'"Sufficiently Cartholic",' suggested James demurely.

'Oh, we're coming on a bit at home, at Blandfield,' said Mary. 'But I'm afraid Eileen, my new young stepmother, would say "the Reverend Freeling".'

'There's no vocative for that,' said Philip. 'Just as well, perhaps. What does "Aunt Eileen" – *puisque tante il y a* – do when she addresses the clergy?'

'It can't often happen,' said Mary. 'Any more than you're likely to have to address your "Aunt Eileen" – and no loss to you. I don't see Father bringing her over to meet Aunt Jane.'

'It doesn't sound suitable.'

'I can just hear Aunt Jane saying "as common as dirt".'

'There, if you'll forgive me, you're being anachronistic,' said Philip. 'That's how our generation talks.'

'I hope not,' said James.

'Prig!' said Philip affectionately. 'Not to all and sundry, but between ourselves. And I'm sure it must be perfectly true.'

'It is indeed,' said Mary.

'You see, we've all got tendencies to euphemism,' said Philip. 'I expect it's a kind instinct. But different generations pick on different disadvantages for their charity. The aunts would say, almost blushing, that Eileen wasn't "quite, quite", or was "rather, rather", or "not out of the top drawer" – as if it were something "not quite nice".'

'And indeed it isn't!' said Mary.

'She'd call you "Padre",' Philip said to James, knowing that this hint of militarism would destroy any sympathy he might have for the wretched Eileen.

'No, our generation is more tender-hearted about blackamoors,' Philip continued. 'At our preparatory school they talked about "Scouts of all colours", do you remember? And they advised us never to refer to "niggers" – a word of which our uncles were rather fond.'

'But they also told us that "a Scout is a brother to every other Scout, no matter to what social class the other belongs".'

'We knew that meant nothing at all,' said Philip. 'The school was advertised as being for "the sons of gentlemen" – and so on the whole it was. The only really common boy is now a newspaper viscount.'

'Some people would think we were being frightfully vulgar,' said James.

'I'm sure they would,' said Philip. 'But you know what I think about "some people"! "Some people" adore being shocked and indignant, and now it's out of date to object to blasphemy or filth, they have to do their best with our little class distinctions.'

'You must be amused at our middle-class snobbery,' said Mary to James.

'Middle class myself,' said James. 'Do you know, once I had the curiosity to look at the table of precedence, and I found I came after any OBE. Rather humiliating.'

'I bet you don't care!'

'I do not. But you, Doctor, a progressive young woman, one would expect you to be dead against class distinctions.'

'I might be, but I've chosen to work for old people. They've seen enough changes, and I don't want any more for them. Let things go on as they are for their lifetime. It's not important, anyway.'

'I feel much the same about my clients,' said Philip. 'One must in a place like this. So science and the law are against progress! What about the Church?'

'I chiefly feel it's no affair of mine,' said James. 'And I'm glad it's not. Besides, on the whole, it's the sorts of clergymen that I don't like who are always writing to the papers about it. I just take what comes. And now it's about time I went to church.'

'Now let's get down to business,' said Mary.

'You needn't have hesitated to begin in front of James,' said Philip. 'What have you to report?'

'What have *you*?'

'I saw Uncle George, of course. He's quite interested in the idea and talks of speaking to Henville-Poke.'

'That old fool would only find a feeble creature who'd give him a few gentle pats,' said Mary. 'I've found an excellent Miss Twistleton.'

'A very good name,' said Philip.

'Oh, for God's sake, Philip don't let's have any more of that silly snob game!'

'You're not very grateful. You recommend the woman, and to please you I say something nice about her name, which is all I know of her. Tell me some more.'

'She's properly qualified. She's trying to work up a practice here, where she has to live with an aged mother.'

'That's sympathetic,' said Philip.

'Why?'

'I have no notion why.'

'You're being maddening,' said Mary. 'But at least you can tell me how to get her into that house. Shall I write a note?'

'No,' said Philip. 'You'd better telephone, then you'll be on firmer ground. They all hate the telephone and feel helpless on it, particularly Aunt Jane, who will probably answer. I feel almost disloyal betraying her to you in this way.'

'Why do it then?'

'Because I'm thinking of Uncle George,' said Philip. 'I hope you will do him good. If there's a conflict of loyalties I support my own sex.'

'You evidently do prefer it,' said Mary unpleasantly.

'I think most self-respecting people get on better with their own sex,' said Philip coldly. 'But of course I have many women clients.'

'I wonder what they think of you,' said Mary.

'They trust me,' said Philip. 'Would you like to ring up now? It's quite a good time.'

Mary went to the telephone and Philip, with a sigh, picked up his sketch-book. Her head was not likely to come in useful to him, but one never knew. At the moment he was illustrating *The Spoils of Poynton,* but he had reason to hope that other novels of Henry James's would be entrusted to him. He had already been obliged to research into costume, and even into the facial differences of a past generation. He was extremely conscientious, for it was his ambition to render the scenes as good contemporary readers could have imagined them, and with more visual accuracy than the Master himself might have summoned to their aid. He wished not only to give the features of the people but to suggest rather more of their characters than could be shown in 'real life'. It ought to be critical and creative work of the greatest interest. Meanwhile he noted down any chance models that came his way in case there might one day be a place for them in the vast *oeuvre*; but as he said to himself, Mary would always look anachronistic.

As he was to hear her telephone conversation from either side, it may as well be thus reported.

'Hullo – oh, it's Miss Elwell. Sorry to bother you. I'm Mary Keyworth. Can I talk to Aunt Jane, please?'

'Yes, I'll fetch my sister.'

'Good afternoon, Mary. Where are you ringing from?'

'From Philip's rooms. I've been telling him about a masseuse I've found for Uncle George. I do hope he'll give her a trial.'

'A masseuse? Wouldn't a man do better?'

'I haven't heard of a suitable man hereabouts – at least not one who will visit patients in their own houses. It's work women do well.'

'Taking a job from a man!'

'She needs a job as much as any man. She has an invalid mother to keep.'

'Oh, poor thing! She sounds a brave woman. Will she stand up to Henville-Poke, do you think?'

'Yes, she's a sensible person, not too young.'

'Is she – er – all right socially?'

'Miss Twistleton? Yes, I should certainly say she was.'

'Of course it's a good name. I'm very grateful to you, Mary. Would you get her to ring us up?'

'Well, now it will depend on Uncle George,' said Philip. 'You've done your best, and with more success than I expected.'

'You'll ring me up, and tell me how things go on?' said Mary.

'Certainly.'

'Well, now I know you're dying to get rid of me.'

'Not at all,' said Philip with almost obvious insincerity. 'You don't mind my drawing? I can listen to you at the same time.'

'You could, if I had anything to say.'

'Well, you'll come again when you're this way?'

'If I stayed any longer now I'd be tempted to tell you what I think about Aunt Jane.'

'I'd much rather you didn't' said Philip.

'You're terribly like her in some ways,' said Mary, almost viciously.

'Of that I'm well aware,' said Philip, hoping to take the wind out of her sails. And then, when she had gone, he settled down more comfortably with his sketch-book.

He was thus occupied when James returned.

'Had a "nice service", my dear, as the Prots would say?'

'Eve of All Saints, procession and all that. 'For all thy saints' he sang in his flat voice.

'What did you wear?'

'Only an alb, naturally.'

'Of course you must all have been in white. I suppose the Vicar preached?'

'As stupid as usual. What about your session with Cousin Mary?'

'She's so nasty that she's quite worthy of being called a cousin,' said Philip. 'Besides, she was "presuming on the connection", as I think people used to say in better days. She was bossy and cantankerous.'

'Odd. She was quite pleasant when I was there.'

'What was she like when you were alone with her, before I came in?'

'Just a bit inquisitive, perhaps,' said James. 'How did I get on with your family? How did I like working in this town? And a bit about our domestic arrangements.'

'I'm sure you made judicious replies. She wouldn't dare to ask you about me, I should hope?'

'Not quite,' said James. 'But she tried to be a little facetious about your being under your Aunt Jane's thumb. She got small change out of me, I can tell you.'

'Thank heaven you're like me there,' said James. 'It's astonishing and horrifying to me how some people – quite nice people otherwise – can make jokes about their closest friends for the amusement of comparative strangers.'

'And if one resents it, they say one can't take a joke.'

'My father was like that,' said Philip. 'An insensitive man. It's a thing Aunt Eliza would be incapable of doing. It's one of the failings of *les anges de la rue*.'

'Mary thinks you're rather like your Aunt Jane.'

'So she said – and she did not mean it as a compliment.'

'You have a look of her,' said James.

'I'm delighted to hear it, and I hope I have an echo of her way of talking. But I would hate to be an angel in the street. I'd far rather be an angel in the house, like Aunt Eliza.'

'That would certainly be more comfortable for me,' said James.

'I'm more cut out for it,' said Philip. 'I find it hard to like people I don't love.'

'Evidently you were quite right when you decided that you hadn't got a vocation to the priesthood.'

'Yes, you have to be liked, poor thing,' said Philip. 'I'd rather begin with a mild indifference or even a slight antipathy on the part of strangers, and then "grow on them", as people say. That is, if they're worth it.'

'A very conceited thing to want to do,' said James. 'You're stiff with spiritual pride, I regret to tell you.'

'*Mea culpa*,' said Philip. 'It's a sort of defence mechanism at work after the visit from Doctor Mary.'

'How else did she try to take you down?'

'She made a faint suggestion of sexual anomaly.'

'Highly impertinent,' said James. 'Of course one knows some so-called "normal people" have a natural repugnance to those who aren't just like themselves. One makes allowances for it. But an educated woman of our generation, a doctor, ought to have got above that sort of thing, or at least above showing it unprovoked.'

'In any case, as she obviously doesn't like me, I don't know why she's cottoned on to me in this way,' said Philip. 'She was quite friendly the other day at the aunts', but I don't see that she really needs my help to prescribe for her own uncle. However, I was willing to be amenable.'

'Perhaps she's an *ange de la rue* and likes strangers. She was all right with me. Now, as you're a sort of cousin, or at least a connection, she can be bitchy and domineering with you.'

'Anyway, I don't suppose we shall see her again.'

9

'What's she like?' asked Philip. 'Aunt Eliza seems to have thought Miss Twistleton quite a nice little person.'

'Your Aunt Eliza is a rotten hand at describing people,' said Jane.

'What are your own impressions?'

'She's short, a bit bunchy – very brown, coat and skirt and hat. Face rather like an apple.'

'Apple-cheeked?'

'Oh no, like a very mature sort of russet apple. I should say she was in her forties, but she looks like one of those people who don't change much. Somewhat rough-cheeked, really, with thickish lips that seem to stick out. She doesn't talk much, but she has quite a pleasant voice.'

'A very suitable appearance for a woman who works hard for her living.'

'She's got a car,' said Jane, as if to qualify Miss Twistleton's claims for sympathy on the ground of impecuniousness.

'She must need that to get about to her patients.'

'She has good, capable-looking hands.'

'Well, that's what matters. What does Uncle George think of her?'

'He seems to take to her, fortunately – and Henville-Poke has given his blessing. Really one feels quite obliged to Mary, poor girl.'

'Why "poor girl"? And she's hardly a girl now.'

'I wonder if she really likes going out to work this way. It's not as if she had to do it, like poor Miss Twistleton. Her father is very well off, and I imagine her mother left her something.'

'I suppose she must like it, or she wouldn't do it. She's really interested in medical science.'

'I think it was probably to get away from home,' said Jane.

'After her mother's death it must have been very disagreeable, and sometimes – I'm afraid – not quite a suitable place for a young girl.'

'I only vaguely remember "Uncle Stanley".'

'Very much the business man, and I think trying to be like the Americans,' said Jane. 'Smokes incessantly, very trying. Once, your Uncle George and I stayed at the same hotel in Buxton with Stanley and poor Mabel, his wife. For a Keyworth family funeral. Stanley smoked through every meal, even with his poached eggs at breakfast.'

'How revolting!' said Philip. 'I should have insisted on separate tables.'

'Well, poor Mabel died when the girl was about sixteen. I'm not surprised that she thought up ways of getting out of that house. First she went to Germany for the language, and then somewhere for medical studies, and now she's on her own.'

'It seems to have worked out very well. I hear her father's married again, which wouldn't make home any more attractive.'

'No, indeed,' said Jane. 'I hear "number two"' – one can call her that as she's vulgar enough – is a dreadful young woman. It's really creditable to Mary to have such good manners, if you think of her background.'

'I dare say she went to a good school, and I believe she was quite a lot with Granny Keyworth, wasn't she?'

'Yes, you were always fond of the old lady. Well, she wasn't your mother-in-law. Try to marry an orphan, and avoid that relationship.'

'Anyway, if I marry, I can't give anyone a mother-in-law.'

'That's a pity – your mother always wanted a daughter.'

'But did she really like in-laws any more than you and Aunt Eliza do?'

'She hadn't got many,' said Jane, and stopped to think. 'No, I don't think she cared about your father's family, and of course she detested your Cousin Rosa.'

'You seem rather to have come round to "Doctor Mary".'

'That's what Miss Tillotson calls her,' said Jane. 'Yes, I don't think she's bad at all.'

'I find her domineering,' said Philip. 'Too bossy altogether.'

'She has to be, to get things done,' said Jane. 'I dare say

63

she'd get rid of that if she married. But I suppose she gets a tendency to it from her grandmother. Things sometimes skip a generation.'

'What was her mother like?'

'Poor Mabel? She was more of a lady than Stanley, or rather less not so, if you see what I mean.'

'I see very well.'

'Pity Stanley didn't take after his mother. She at least was a lady, and her mother was an honourable. What are you laughing at?'

'Odd – I don't know why you made me think of that nasty murderer, Sidney Harry Fox. Do you remember he tried to style himself "the Honourable", and when he was asked what claim he had to that distinction he said: "My mother's father was a gentleman."'

'I don't see how he could have been. She used to connive with her son in bilking lodging-houses, didn't she?' said Jane. 'Then he stifled her for the insurance money.'

'How we love the murderers of England!' said Philip. 'They're our personal mythology.'

'I don't quite know what you mean,' said Jane. 'But we do find them useful when we want to illustrate a point.'

'I remember another thing about Fox, but it's rather macabre,' said Philip. 'I thought of it the other day when I saw Uncle George's teeth on the dining-room table. When the jury had been out for some time, they sent for Mrs Fox's false teeth.'

'Don't!' said Jane.

George came in, this time wearing his teeth, and in general he presented a better cared-for appearance.

'Getting on much better, old chap,' he said to Philip. 'But it's rather a grind at first.'

'You must persevere,' said Jane. 'Miss Tillotson has done you a lot of good already. But you must go on, and not back.'

Philip perceived that Miss Twistleton had at once been elevated to the category of those who can do no wrong and that, typically, his aunts had got her name wrong. That was encouraging, for they frequently did it with names they most often used.

It was time for him to go, and he saw Eliza in the drive. He let her in as he went out: neither of his aunts ever carried a latchkey.

'I'm sorry Kate Springfield delayed me,' said Eliza. 'I was recommending her to try Miss Tillotson, who's done so much for your uncle.'

Philip walked home with a much lighter heart than he had had the week before. Miss Twistleton seemed to have come to the house bringing peace in her little bag. There might not be love in that household, but now there was peace, its best consequence. Peace was precious even without love, while love without peace was murderous, bloody, full of blame: it led to possessiveness and scenes and people throwing plates at each other's heads, like D.H. Lawrence. One had read of it, and caught glimpses of it. 'God preserve me from it!' said Philip.

'You've missed a visitor,' said James, who for once had been indulging in an afternoon at home. 'You'll hardly guess who it was.'

'The Vicar?'

'No, your cousin, Doctor Mary.'

'What on earth brought her here?'

'That is what I've been asking myself, and I've been unable to find an answer.'

'I conclude she gave you no clue?'

'Not much of one. I felt more as if she were searching for an excuse to give me. She said she looked in because she was passing.'

'Whence and whither?'

'She did not vouchsafe.'

'I hope she isn't going to make a habit of it,' said Philip. 'But I shouldn't think she is often this way. Perhaps she's great friends with her cousin Derek.'

'She could have come from Madingfold, but she wasn't going there. She wants you to ring her up in London any time after eight.'

'If people ask one to ring them up, it's usually about something of no interest to oneself,' said Philip. 'If it's interesting to her, she can ring up, if she likes.'

'She said she thought you were selfish.'

'Oh, so you had quite a nice little talk about me?'

'She did most of the talking, I need hardly say. She didn't think you saw enough people.'

'Gracious! With my clients, and the clerk, and old Dolmidge, not to speak of you and Miss Snape and Doris, I must see at least a dozen people every day – and quite often my aunts as well. It's as much as I can manage.'

'I don't think Mary would count any of us.'

'What would she count? Duchesses and smart people?'

'I don't think so,' said James. 'She said you were a snob, but seemed to approve when I said you never were a social climber.'

'But she herself seemed to enjoy our little snobbish talk,' said Philip. 'After all, if a naturalist is interested in small differences between flora and fauna, why shouldn't a human naturalist – if there is such an expression, as there ought to be – be interested in small social distinctions?'

'Why not indeed?' said James. 'I wouldn't even blame him if he climbed in search of rare specimens.'

'I expect she went away saying that we were interested in nothing else,' said Philip. 'Just because we didn't happen to talk about eschatology or stamp-collecting. People are like that. But whom did she think I ought to know?'

'"Interesting people",' said James drily.

'Oh, my God, don't I know!' said Philip. 'Authors, artists, people interested in Causes – all seething with hatred and jealousy of one another when they're not popping in and out of each other's beds. What a lot one is spared if one is contentedly provincial! Anyway, what business is it of hers?'

'Oh, you know how women love saying of a man that he's "wasting his talents",' said James. 'Besides, she had to make some conversation as I gave her tea.'

'We've another visitor coming,' said James, after a pause.

'Damn!' said Philip. 'Who is it?'

'It's Oliver. He rang up and invited himself to a drink. He should be here in no time.'

'What's he doing here?'

'Oh, he's been lunching with someone of importance, I suppose, or he's going to dine with someone of importance.'

'Would Mary count him as an "interesting person"?'

'I don't want to be hard on him, but she might.'

Oliver Hutton had been up at Oxford with them. He was now a very superior sort of travel agent. He and his partners had an office just off Bond Street where they arranged 'luxury travel' for some of their clients and 'unusual travel' for others. Oliver and one of the partners did a good deal of travelling themselves to keep their information up to date. He had probably come to this place (a dormitory for London) to pass Saturday to Monday with some magnate for whom he was to hire a villa or a yacht. His life was therefore extremely unlike that of Philip or James, for whom he had a friendly contempt. Philip found him entertaining, and had sometimes accompanied him on short jaunts; James disliked him intensely.

He came in, spry and condescending. 'Still in your little corner, my dears? "The world forgetting by the world forgot"?'

'Alas, "the world is too much with us",' replied Philip. 'My clients and James's lads.'

'Lads?'

'Church lads, Oliver. And their sisters and their cousins and their aunts.'

'It doesn't sound very exciting,' said Oliver.

'Why should it be?' said James.

'Well, you're two intelligent people,' said Oliver. 'Aren't you being wasted in this little backwater, or whatever you like to call it?'

'If we didn't do our jobs here, someone else would have to do them,' said James. 'The people here have souls, as Newman said of the people of Birmingham.'

'And they have property too, and they often want me to take care of it,' said Philip.

'That I find easier to believe,' said Oliver. 'But less qualified people could do your jobs. There's a need for clever people like you.'

'Oh, my dear, can't you arrange all the travels of the rich for them?' said Philip.

'That's not all,' said Oliver. 'More clever people are needed who'd be acceptable to "the rich", as you call them. Do you mean to stay here for ever?'

'We've sometimes thought of making a change,' said James.

'Well, you'd better think quickly,' said Oliver. 'The world isn't going to stay still much longer, and it's not at all certain which way the cat will jump – though I'm sure you read the liberal weeklies, and don't imagine there's another side.'

'Not a very nice side,' said Philip.

'Both sides are repellent,' said James.

Shortly afterwards James was called away.

'But you, Philip, how do you manage?' said Oliver. 'I rather gather there's "nothing there shouldn't be" between you and James any more?'

'He's a priest,' said Philip coldly.

'Oh, my dear, getting about the world as I do, I've met plenty of naughty clergymen,' said Oliver.

'I've no doubt, but I don't like them. Nor does James.'

'But he can't expect you to be a vestal.'

'We never speak of it,' said Philip. 'And I don't mean to speak of it now. If there were anything to speak of – as there could be, of course – James would rather not know.'

'You mean, it might hurt him?'

'That, I think, he wouldn't mind. He'd accept it as a penance. And he might like to know that I felt free.'

'I don't begin to understand.'

'I never expected you to.'

'Then why can't you and James talk about it in a civilized way?'

'He wouldn't want either to condemn or condone.'

'What hypocrisy! Of course he condones.'

'Not really. He never *knows*, though he may think it probable. I think people make too much fuss about "condoning" – and throw the word about much more than we do in my profession. Look at the people who have scruples about going to Italy in case they're "condoning" the invasion of Ethiopia! And I expect there are people who would say you are "condoning" all sorts of horrors because some of your clients may very likely entertain Nazi leaders in the villas you hire for them.'

'I have heard it said.'

'You are only responsible for your clients being comfortable in the villa you get for them, for their treating it well, and paying for it,' said Philip. 'That's as far as your intention goes, and it's unlikely that your knowledge goes much further.'

'You do rather lay down the law, but I suppose it's your job,' said Oliver. 'And yet I rather feel that if I invited you to join Larborough's party in the Riviera for Christmas you wouldn't accept?'

'Thank you, but I'd rather not come,' said Philip. 'I shouldn't think it wrong, but uncongenial. Do you really have to get him guests as well as everything else?'

'So and so many of either sex,' said Oliver. 'Just as I have to buy so and so many yards of red morocco and blue morocco for his library. I don't think I'll wait for James, if you'll excuse me to him. There's your telephone.'

It was only half-past eight, and already Mary was asking why he had not rung up to tell her how Miss Twistleton was being received.

10

'I'm sorry, but I can't really say that I like Oliver,' said James next morning. He had returned from church, and was sitting down to breakfast.

'He has a horrid job,' said Philip. 'But I suppose he doesn't dislike it, and he can't be blamed for it.'

'No – but think of the sort of people he has to deal with,' said James. '"Evil communications corrupt good manners", as St Paul saith.'

'They do indeed. The bloom has been rubbed off Oliver.'

'But who keeps it?' said James. 'I'm afraid it's only a matter of degree. Even in our "backwater", as Oliver calls it, we're occasionally forced into compromise, and have to justify ourselves by a bit of casuistry.'

'No harm in that,' said Philip. 'In my profession we have case law as well as precept law, and all sorts of loopholes – so why shouldn't you?'

'The parallel isn't quite exact,' said James. 'But it's a pity the word "casuistry" has come to be used with a bad meaning. After all, it's an honourable and useful part of moral science. It ought to help ordinary people to lead decent lives in this complicated and rather evil world. They have to compromise.'

'One hardly knows any uncompromisingly good people,' said Philip.

'That's why your aunts give me a sort of pointer in life, as I said once before,' said James. 'They're magnificently uncompromising.'

'Yes, they can get on without compromise themselves,' said Philip. 'But you should hear Aunt Eliza defending the inconsistencies of some Tory politician. A model of casuistry.'

'And I dare say they are quite severe on less favoured people.'

'I'm afraid, James, that you'd find them frequently and horribly guilty of harsh judgements then. They're always so afraid of condoning or encouraging evil that they go too far the other way.'

'Yes, the golden mean is to be sought, I suppose,' said James. 'But I'd rather err on the side of charity.'

'I forgot to tell you, Oliver invited me to join Lord Larborough's Christmas party somewhere on the Riviera.'

'As you forgot to mention it, I take it you refused.'

'Naturally. Anyway I shall have luncheon with my aunts on Christmas Day. Won't you come?'

'Thank you, but I expect I shall just have time to go up to London to see my parents. Would you refuse to meet Larborough?'

'Not if it was too late. I mean if I found myself in the same room.'

'I quite agree. I don't think one should ever be so priggish or unkind,' said James. 'Of course if someone blasphemed...'

'You could stalk out, you're tall enough,' said Philip. 'If I were to flounce out, I should only be absurd.'

'You oughtn't to mind that, in a good cause,' said James with a smile.

'But I should make the good cause absurd,' said Philip. 'By the way, Doctor Mary telephoned to reproach me for not having rung her up. Why this feminine coyness? She's a doctor, and nearly a cousin, and quite two inches taller than I am. I'm hanged if I'm going to be *aux petits soins* with her.'

'You don't think she's up to something?'

'I can't imagine what,' said Philip. 'Unless she's taken a fancy to you. That would be a bore for you.'

'It would be a worse bore if it were for you,' said James. 'Your family would be involved in one way or another.'

'In every possible way,' said Philip. 'But there's no fear of that.'

Mary's subsequent telephone conversation with Jane was reported to him on his next visit.

'Mary seems cross with you,' said Jane.

71

'I can't think why she should be,' said Philip.

'She'd expected you to ring her up and tell her about Miss Tillotson.'

'I suppose that's why she came to see us the other day. I was here, so she had tea with James.'

'She asked me to scold you.'

'Well, we can take that as done, can't we? I hope Miss Twistleton is still being a success?'

'Your uncle seems pleased. She's such a heavy woman, I should think she could give him quite drastic massage.'

'So you could satisfy Mary?'

'I'm not so sure about that,' said Jane. 'What's she up to? She seems to have cottoned on to you two.'

'If she's interested in James Freeling she's laying herself out for disappointment.'

'Is he under a vow not to marry?' asked Jane. 'I thought clergy in the Church of England could do what they liked.'

'Not a vow. A resolution, perhaps. There's a very old tradition in favour of celibacy.'

'I shouldn't think it cost him much,' said Jane, who sometimes surprised him and startled him by her acuteness.

'Perhaps she's interested in you,' said Eliza.

'Oh, I hope not. Better James. He's her own size, and protected by his cassock.'

'It mightn't be such a bad thing,' said Eliza.

'Of course it would be much worse for me than for anyone else if it came to a point,' said Philip. 'But both of you would dislike it very much indeed.'

'Oh, come!' said Eliza. 'She's a very nice girl, and quite well brought up, considering. A bit tall, perhaps.'

'And being rather short, you can't pick and choose,' said Jane nastily. 'You may have to take what you can get.'

'You shouldn't assume I could "get" Mary if I liked,' said Philip. 'And I don't like.'

'People can't always have what they like,' said Jane, snorting.

'But they can avoid what they don't like, and I generally do.'

'Anyway, it's high time you settled down,' said Jane. 'It would be good for the practice too.'

'I'm not going to sacrifice myself to the practice, I'd sooner

72

sacrifice the practice to me. I may like to leave the firm at any time, and I certainly don't intend to marry.'

'What your grandfather would have said!' exclaimed Jane. 'He was so proud of the family firm.'

'Who cares what he would have said?'

'You ought to,' said Eliza. 'He was very much attached to you when you were small.'

'So, I'm to arrange my life so that it would have pleased a vain old man who wanted to be a sort of patriarch?' said Philip. 'Think for a minute. You can't honestly believe that I'm under any obligation to him, even if he did pat me on the head when I was a baby and give me a rattle. He loved me because he thought I would continue his line – it was purely selfish.'

'Anyway, you'll ring Mary up?' said Jane. 'She seemed to expect it'

'Perhaps,' said Philip. 'But if I do I must have something to say to her. When shall I see Miss Twistleton?'

'If you wait a little, you may see her at any moment now,' said Jane. 'She's taken your uncle, and the old dog, if you please, for a drive over the forest.'

'How very nice! It will do Danny good to get a bit of a run.'

'It won't do your uncle any good to catch his death pottering after him.'

'I'm sure George is very well wrapped up,' said Eliza.

'I hope so,' said Jane, ignoring the sarcasm. 'And I hope Miss Tillotson is a careful driver.'

A few minutes later George was heard at the door. Unlike Jane and Eliza he carried a latchkey, perhaps an assertion of masculinity. He held the old dog wrapped in a pink blanket and cooed over him: 'Dear little dog, warm as a little toastie.'

'Wouldn't Miss Tillotson come in?' said Jane.

'She had to go to another patient.'

'I hoped to meet her,' said Philip.

'You shall, if you'll come with us on Sunday. I want to look at my old home at Crampton. Miss Twistleton will pick you up on her way here. Would half-past ten do?'

'Thank you, very nicely.'

'We'll take a picnic of sorts and eat it in the car, as it will be too cold for anything else,' said George, and retired upstairs with the dog.

'This is a new development,' said Philip. 'How very lucky

you seem to be in Miss Twistleton. How good of her to give all that time to driving Uncle George about.'

'He pays for the petrol,' said Jane sourly.

'I should hope so,' said Eliza. 'She's got her living to make.'

'I've never seen Crampton,' said Philip. 'It's quite near Freeling. James will be interested.'

'Can't you take him?' said Eliza.

'I'm sure he's got other services,' said Jane hastily.

'Unfortunately he has,' said Philip. 'He's preaching at eleven o'clock.'

'You might pass Comstead,' said Jane. 'You could ask after your Cousin Rosa, who's very ill. Bertie wrote a quite uncontrolled letter to your uncle. He said he was in "sore distress".'

'I don't know his usual style,' said Philip, 'but I should guess that meant she was dying. You'd better look out your mourning.'

'My dear boy!' protested Jane. 'Anyhow half-mourning will do very well for her.'

'Philip's gone off to St Simon's, *I* know,' said Jane.

'You talk as if it were some shocking dissipation,' said Eliza.

'So it is, rather, at this time of day,' said Jane. 'I don't like a man to be too churchy. I'd like to get him away from St Simon's and Mr Freeling.'

'I think it's very nice that he should be a good churchman.'

'Yes, but one can go too far. He even goes to confession, he told me.'

'Not to Father Freeling, I imagine.'

'No, to St John's, to old Canon Robson. He must be pretty surprised. It's a new departure in our family.'

'I'm sure Canon Robson takes it in his stride.'

'And this serving at the altar, or whatever they call it,' said Jane. 'It's very undignified at his age. What can his clients think? They even give him quite menial jobs to do at St Simon's when they're short of servers.'

'What d'you mean?'

'Well, carrying the cross, for example.'

Eliza laughed. 'I don't think you know what you're saying.'

'Well, I'm sure marriage would put an end to that. I don't think any woman would care to see her husband carrying the cross.'

'Mary, on the other hand, probably doesn't believe a thing,' said Eliza. 'Scientists usually don't.'

'Then things might equalize out between them,' said Jane. 'I've had an idea. I shall telephone to Mary (as I'm sure Philip won't) and tell her about this picnic. She ought to be interested in Crampton, her father's old home – and I rather fancy she was at that grand girls' school at Freeling.'

'You'd think she'd have come out with it.'

'She might not. Anyhow, if she happens to be here this coming weekend it might interest her to suggest herself, or just to go on her own. That's why I didn't like your bringing in Mr Freeling.'

'Really, Jane! One can't interfere with other people's affairs to that extent.'

'I'm not going to interfere in the least. She wants to know about Miss Tillotson and I shall say how pleased we are, and how kind she is to George – and just mention their plans. They're not a secret.'

'Do you think George or Philip would want her there? Can't you leave people alone?'

'Nothing happens if you do.'

'I do think people should be left to manage their own affairs,' said Eliza.

'Of course it's much easier and pleasanter to leave people alone,' said Jane.

'I'm afraid you'd never find it easy or pleasant,' said Eliza.

'The aunts seem to have taken a turn in favour of Mary,' said Philip.

'I expect they think I'm in the way,' said James.

'Aunt Jane probably does. Aunt Eliza would think it a sin of presumption to have such an idea about a clergyman.'

'And perhaps I am in the way?'

'Not in Mary's way,' said Philip. 'Dear James, I've often told you I don't know what I'd do without you, and it's true. But I do know one or two things I wouldn't do.'

'She's not so bad,' said James, who could afford to be generous.

'She's all right for people who like women like that. But I've no wish to get married in general, or to marry her in particular. And I'm sure she'd say the same about me.'

'Yes, I do think your aunts are building up a story on no foundation. Doctor Mary is just a rather bossy woman who likes to have a finger in every pie.'

'That's what I think, too.'

'And "Mr Philip and Dr Mary Milsom" wouldn't sound right.'

'But that's the charm of the whole thing from the aunts' point of view – or rather Aunt Jane's, which counts the most. Mary might give up being a doctor if she married – "so unfeminine". And if I married I couldn't afford to chuck the office. I'm sure they've thought of that. A way of killing two birds with one stone.'

'Interfering old ladies.'

'Oh, I'm sure they have no idea that they want to interfere in our lives – still less to ruin them.'

'Even the Almighty could hardly interfere more.'

'Well, luckily they're not almighty.'

'Don't you be too sure of that!' said James.

'Yes, what dreadful faults the divine attributes would be, if they were possessed by human beings. Imagine if they were omniscient!'

'As far as you're concerned, I expect they nearly are.'

11

Miss Twistleton corresponded exactly to Jane's description. 'Mr Philip', she called him, which at first took him aback. Then he realized that it was because his uncle must often have talked about him. 'Philip, Philip' – she could hardly have replied all the time with 'Mr Milsom' or 'your nephew'.

'I expect your aunts will already have started for church,' she said. And indeed it was George who opened the door and carried out the old dog wrapped in his pink blanket. He had caught the custom of the house; Jane and Eliza, who had been brought up 'not to keep the horses waiting', were always dead on time for an expected car.

George settled down next to Miss Twistleton, entrusting Danny to Philip at the back.

'Your Cousin Rosa died on Thursday,' said George.

'I suppose Aunt Jane and Aunt Eliza are very black,' said Philip.

'More than there's any occasion for, they complained. Their half-mourning is mostly too light and summery.'

'"She should have died hereafter",' said Philip. 'But I expect they've been busy altering and adapting.'

'Oh yes, snip, snip, snip. And the morning-room floor covered with bits of black or grey,' said George. 'By the way, we're not to pass through Comstead.'

'I bet Aunt Jane said: "It would be too sad"!'

'She did. But there are practical reasons. If any of that family were to catch a glimpse of us they would think that, if we could get so far today, we could very well get there for the funeral tomorrow.'

'That would never do.'

'We've written, of course,' said George. 'They said "no flowers", or rather "only family flowers". So of course there

77

has been a great debate whether we are close enough family or not.'

'The noes had it, I hope?'

'Yes,' said George. 'Very well argued by your Aunt Eliza, and with my casting vote.'

'Anyway, I'm not near enough to have to wear a black tie, supposing I were wearing a tie,' said Philip, who wore a high-necked sweater.

'I do like to see people sensibly dressed for a day in the country,' said Miss Twistleton, who seemed to be a person of few words.

'One of those horrid Comstead cousins, I think it was Peter – the naval one, you know – once looked me up and down scornfully and said: "I don't think anyone who's worn uniform would care to wear *that*."'

'Odious cub!' said George. 'Just like that family. Their idea of pleasure used to be to go to a third-rate musical comedy in full evening dress.'

'Well, they can have a good show tomorrow,' said Philip. 'I'm sure they didn't say "no mourning".'

Now they had passed through a fringe of the forest and entered farming country, that of George's youth. Ploughed fields crisp with rime, black skeletons of trees elegantly traceried against the duck's egg blue of the sky, mellow brick oast-houses. Soon they would be in the three parishes where once George had been 'Master George' to everyone.

'I don't suppose there's anyone still alive to call me that,' he wondered sadly. 'I don't want us to get to Crampton till they are out of church,' he continued. 'Let's take the road by Freeling first.'

Soon it was before them, a hideous mansion, on a smaller scale strongly reminiscent of St Pancras Station. James was very well out of it.

'Look!' said Miss Twistleton, indicating a small dark-blue car. 'Isn't that Doctor Mary's runabout?'

'What brings her here?' said George.

'"Oh, my prophetic soul, my aunt!"' exclaimed Philip.

'She's stopped,' said George. 'Will you bring her over here, Philip? We've plenty of food, if she likes to join our picnic.'

'You don't seem very pleased to see me,' said Mary, in her most irritating 'little-girl' voice.

'Surprise is still my dominant emotion,' said Philip. 'I was wondering what chance brought you here – what good wind, should I say?'

'*You* didn't invite me,' she said petulantly.

'It wasn't my picnic. And if Uncle George did, he seems to have forgotten. He's said nothing about it.'

'It was Aunt Jane, of all people.'

'Indeed!'

'Not that she invited me, but she told me where you were going. As I happened to be coming down this weekend I thought I might as well join you. I can show you a bit more of Freeling. I'm an old girl.'

'Well, that will be very nice,' said Philip. 'Something to tell James.'

Mary pouted, but took a place at the back of the car while Philip moved the old dog into the space between them.

Danny growled.

'Oh, Danny, we're not going to bark at Cousin Mary, are we?' said Philip with deliberate fatuousness.

'I suppose I ought to leave a card on the headmistress,' she said.

When she alighted for this purpose, Philip also got out, for she was to show him the chapel.

'I believe it used to be the billiard-room,' she said. 'Hideous, isn't it?'

'And what my aunts would call "abysmally low", and so should I.'

'The ballroom has become the great hall for assemblies and exams,' she said. 'Uncle George will remember its splendours in the time of Sir Aldebert and Lady Alethea.'

'I expect it was even uglier then.'

'The family were always buried at Crampton,' said George. 'We'll see their monuments in the church. I thought we might dare to eat our luncheon in the porch.'

'I can do better for you than that,' said Mary. 'I rang up, and we can use the surgery. We want to be warm, and it's a chance for a little conference, isn't it, Miss Twistleton?'

They drove for the mile and a half's distance in the two cars, and reunited in the churchyard.

'This reminds me, I was sorry to hear you'd had a loss,' said Mary.

79

'Too kind of you,' said Philip. 'It wasn't much loss to any of us.'

'Poisonous woman,' said George.

'I remember dancing with one of the sons,' said Mary, rather taken aback. 'Peter, wasn't it – the naval officer? A very good-looking boy – and awfully nice, I thought.'

They went into the church and noted the Freeling monuments all emblazoned with the chevron and bezants of their arms, from a seventeenth-century altar tomb with recumbent effigies to a Pre-Raphaelite angel weeping over the tablet that commemorated the virtues of Sir Aldebert and Lady Alethea.

The Keyworths had occupied Crampton Manor for only a quarter of a century, and had left no memorial except the sad little grave in the churchyard of Alfred, who had come between George and Stanley, and had died in infancy. The house, however, was grey and dignified in its simple lines. They looked over the wall at the place where the boys had had their own little gardens, and George pointed out a tree overlooking a neighbouring yard. As a boy he had climbed it, to watch a pig being killed, and had fallen out of it, vomiting.

Now Mary took charge of the proceedings. The surgery was at her disposal, and she produced her own very sensible contributions to the picnic: an outsize Thermos flask full of excellent coffee, and a quiche lorraine. Miss Twistleton had promptly transformed herself from George's masseuse into Mary's assistant, and the two men found themselves completely in the doctor's hands. If there were to be a conference, they were not likely to pull their weight. Philip began to think his Aunt Jane was going to be hoist with her own petard.

At once this was only too evident. Mary immediately entered into a speech for the prosecution against the aunts and their household, to the great discomfort of Philip, who was exposed to a conflict of loyalties of a kind so painfully acute that he could hardly hope to come out of it with an unsullied conscience. The fact that George was Jane's husband restrained her to some extent – but she was not noticeably restrained.

'He's of no account in that house,' said Mary, apparently addressing herself to Philip. She began by inveighing against his room; a wretched room facing north, the worst in the house.

'It used to be my grandmother's room,' said Philip mildly. 'I remember as a child in the night nursery – the door being left ajar to give me courage – seeing zigzags of light on the ceiling as Gran went up to bed with her lamp. They hadn't yet got electric light. I've always known what Edith Sitwell meant by "creaking light".'

'No more of your red herrings, Philip, *if* you please,' said Mary. 'No one is interested in your reminiscences.' And she went on to attack the neglect suffered by George in that household – his nasty, ill-prepared meals, while the sisters ate their delicate little messes; the servants' deliberate tardiness in answering his bell, while Philip all the time was cosseted and made much of.

'That has often embarrassed me,' Philip had to admit.

And yet George had never been allowed visits from his own flesh and blood till Mary herself stormed the gate – but Philip was there all the time.

'I wanted him,' said George. 'He's almost like a son. We've seen him grow up. Derek is nothing to me in comparison.'

'Whose fault is that?' said Mary.

'Mine,' said George. 'If it is a fault. Philip's mother was my very dear friend and sister. I've never been at all close to Norman, and I had no use whatever for poor Winnie, Derek's mother.'

Mary was momentarily deflated. 'All the same, something must be done,' she said. 'That wretched room of Uncle George's...'

'*Not* a very nice sickroom,' contributed Miss Twistleton loyally.

Philip then spoke of Eliza's plan.

'Very nice, if Philip's Aunt Jane allows it,' said George sarcastically.

'Oh, I think she can be prevailed upon,' said Philip.

Meanwhile Mary had suggestions for the time when the change was to be made.

'You wouldn't care to go to Madingfold, Uncle George, or to come to us?'

He would not indeed.

Why shouldn't he go to the Forest Hotel for a week or two

after Christmas? It wouldn't be too far for Miss Twistleton to go there and continue his treatment, and Henville-Poke might allow him to consult a specialist who lived in the hotel. Everyone seemed to think there was much to be said for this plan.

'Now I'm going to take Philip from you,' said Mary. 'There will be details to talk over. I'm sure Danny can spare him.'

'Philip, dear, we really have to collaborate,' she said. 'You must support Miss Elwell in her efforts at home while I, with the help of Hilda Twistleton, get Uncle George away for a bit.'

'Is Miss Twistleton likely to have any influence?'

'Yes, in her quiet way she's a very determined woman. And I've thought Miss Elwell really wanted to be fair to Uncle George.'

'Aunt Eliza is always fair to everyone – that is, to everyone she knows. She may be totally unfair to people she only reads about in the newspaper, but does that matter?'

'*You* wouldn't think so, I'm sure.'

'No, I should not.'

'You don't take much notice of the world around you, do you?'

'I make sketches of some of it,' answered Philip.

'Tchah!' said Mary. 'But you don't care for any cause?'

'I can't draw a cause,' said Philip.

'I can't make you out. You're educated, and yet you seem to have grown up in a sort of enclave with those women. Was Aunt Jane cruel to you when you were small?'

'Not really,' said Philip. 'But I do remember one rather odd thing she did. My mother was alive then. She beat me on the hand with a ruler – quite gently. She said she was going to do it harder every day. It was to teach me to bear pain, before I went to school.'

'Was it any help to you?'

'No, it was soon given up. But I can bear pain as well as another.'

'How could your mother have entrusted you to that sadistic, frustrated woman...'

'You're talking like a vulgar newspaper article, and about my aunt,' said Philip. 'My mother loved her, and so do I. I think I'd like you to put me down here. It's not far for me to walk home.'

'Sorry, I'm afraid I went rather too far,' said Mary. 'I flew off the handle.'

'You don't understand her, you see. It needs a little imagination.'

'So you'll let me drive you home?'

'I always meant to,' said Philip with a smile. 'But let's not talk.'

They parted in front of his lodgings.

'Won't you come up for tea?'

'No thanks,' said Mary. 'I really must get back. But I'm forgiven, I hope, old boy?'

'Naturally,' said Philip, shaking hands with formality.

'Well,' said James, 'how did it go?'

'Really, I hardly know,' said Philip, who had explained Mary's intrusion on the picnic. 'She's so extraordinary – first one thing, then another.'

'You mean custom cannot stale her infinite variety?' said James with a smile.

'God preserve me from being accustomed to her!' said Philip. 'As for variety, I saw three very trying versions of her today. I hope there are no more to come. First she was coy, rather "little girlish" and called me "Philip dear". Then she was a virago, making a diatribe against Aunt Jane.'

'Very embarrassing for you.'

'I soon put a stop to that. She was driving me back, and I asked her to put me down and said I'd rather walk home. Of course she apologized and I stayed. Not that I'd ever intended to do anything else.'

'Naturally, though you could probably have cadged a lift from someone. But your aunts wouldn't have liked it.'

'Finally she behaved as if we were "chums" or "pals" or whatever dreadful word she would have used. And she called me "old boy".'

'How did you respond to that?'

'With a formal handshake. It seemed the right thing.'

'I suppose she's trying out these personalities on you to see which works best,' said James. 'Has it struck you she may be afraid of you?'

'Perhaps that's why she likes you better. Parsons don't bite.'

A few days later, to their bewilderment, a cardboard box full of fudge arrived. In it was a card: 'A peace-offering. M.L.K.'

'I don't think we need trouble to have it analysed,' said Philip. 'But I shall not try it on the dog.'

'Anyhow, you said she made a good quiche – if it was her own work,' said James. 'There must be some good in her.'

12

Philip dropped into tea with his aunts rather late one afternoon in the week. They were triumphantly in mourning, and Miss Springfield was there.

'Have you seen this stuff about your Cousin Rosa in the local paper?' asked Jane.

'"Adored by her large, happy family,"' read Kate Springfield sarcastically, '"and deeply respected in Comstead, where she was indefatigable in doing good". She must have fatigued them all right!'

'No one could have respected her who knew her past,' said Jane.

'Oh, she'd had time to live it down, and most people knew nothing about it,' said Miss Springfield. 'It wasn't for that that one disliked her so much. "The rose-covered coffin was carried on the shoulders of her four gallant sons, all officers in the armed forces." Can't you just see it?'

'It must have been too sad,' said Jane.

'It wouldn't have been for me!' said Kate.

'Kate!' protested Eliza. 'Isn't it rather *soon* to talk like that?'

'"And all our sympathy goes to him who said, 'the light has gone out of my life',"' Kate concluded.

'Poor Bertie!' said Eliza. 'I dare say we shall see more of him now – not that I want to.'

'I hope we shan't see any more of the gallant sons,' said Philip.

'They're brave, I suppose,' said Jane, tossing her head contradictorily.

'I dare say they would be, if there were any occasion for it,' said Philip. 'But I find them uncouth.'

'You're as bad as your Uncle George,' said Jane. 'He refuses to see any good in them. Not that his nephew is any better.'

85

'I don't see that that disqualifies him from criticizing the Comstead crowd,' said Philip. 'And I'm told Derek Keyworth has turned out far better than was expected.'

'He's just got engaged,' said Kate. 'I forget her name, but she's an honourable. Norman will enjoy that.'

Then Kate had to go to take Musso out. He had not accompanied her because he did not get on with Danny; unfortunately she had not known that the latter animal would be out in the car with George and Miss Twistleton.

'What a treasure she is!' said Kate. 'I suppose they're having tea in the forest?'

'And George can have his black Indian tea,' said Jane, forgetting that this was also Kate's preference, and had not been indulged.

'I don't know why you don't give him a little pot here,' she was provoked into saying.

'He has one for breakfast,' said Eliza. 'We ought to remember at tea-time too. Everyone doesn't share our love for Lapsang.'

When Kate had gone, Philip opened the subject of Mary. 'Why did you send her after us on Sunday?' he asked Jane reproachfully.

'How was I to know she would go?' said Jane in an injured tone. 'I had no reason to suppose she would be this way again.'

'True,' said Philip. 'Then why should it interest her where we were going?'

'I wanted to tell her about Miss Twistleton, and there was no secret about your plans. Weren't you pleased to see her?'

'Miss Twistleton might have been. Uncle George and I find her a bit overbearing, and Danny doesn't like her at all.'

'What does Danny know about it?'

'You've always said: "Dogs always know." Besides, she insisted on driving me home. I don't think he liked the party being broken up.'

'Why did she do that?'

'Oh, she wanted to talk about your plan for giving this room to Uncle George, and turning his room into the morning-room.'

'*My* plan?'

Philip delicately winked at Eliza. 'Yes, wasn't it your plan?

I can't have dreamt it. You thought it would be such a good thing to spare him the stairs.'

'I never thought of that before,' said Jane surprisingly. 'But it mightn't be such a bad idea. But where's he to go while we change things round? Both rooms want redecorating. He hasn't got his mother to go to now.'

'One of the brothers?' suggested Eliza.

'Mary suggested it, but he turned it down,' said Philip. 'Then she was rather in favour of the Forest Hotel. They specialize in invalids, and there's a resident doctor.'

'Well, perhaps after Christmas,' said Jane. 'Mary's a thoughtful girl.'

She left the room to look for something, and Philip was able to have a word with Eliza.

'Don't let Aunt Jane make too much of Mary, for her own sake,' he said.

'Do you think she's false? She's a bit what I call "smarmy".'

'Not exactly. Or, perhaps, yes – in a way. They will never get on together. They're like oil and vinegar.'

'What's wrong with Mary?'

'Oh, I don't want to find fault. I don't mean there's anything wrong in herself, but everything wrong in her for Aunt Jane. I do beg you to believe me. It isn't just to protect myself from having Mary suggested to me as a wife. I can look after myself all right, and she wouldn't be in the least interested.'

'I don't know about that. She may be fond of you,' said Eliza.

'I don't think so for a moment, and it doesn't matter anyway,' said Philip desperately. 'What does matter is that she dislikes Aunt Jane intensely.'

'Then it would never do,' said Eliza, at once convinced.

Jane returned, and came at once to the point. 'I don't think, Philip, you realize how attached Mary is to you.'

'I'm sure she's not. She's often very rude.'

'Oh, that's her modern way, I expect,' said Jane. 'You're meant to see through it. Really I don't know why you don't propose to her. I'm sure you could be happy together.'

'I'm sure she'd refuse,' said Philip. 'But I shan't risk it!'

'Oh no, she wouldn't,' said Jane. 'Men are so imperceptive. A woman knows.'

'I'll tell you what a man knows about Mary,' said Philip firmly. 'She may or may not want to be married – I don't think she does, myself – but if she is, she will try to domineer her husband. If he submits, she'll despise him. If he doesn't, she'll fight him.'

'I'm not so sure,' said Jane. 'And in many ways it would be suitable. Old Mrs Keyworth would have liked to have you for a grandson.'

'So she had, in the only way that mattered.'

'And that family is much better than it was. I believe Derek is making a good marriage.'

'Well, really! You've never been keen on the Madingfold connection.'

'And Mary's sensible.'

'Perhaps,' said Philip, and then he had an inspiration. 'Haven't you ever thought how dangerous it is to marry a doctor? He can so easily put you to sleep for ever?'

'What an idea!' said Eliza, now venturing to put in a word.

'Don't you know marriage is always considered a sufficient motive for murder?' said Philip. 'The first suspect is nearly always the widow or widower. The law may be an ass at times, but not then. Suppose Mary got tired of her husband, and didn't want a divorce because it might do harm to her practice?'

'Yes, one does know of dreadful cases,' said Jane, and she and Philip delightedly recited their litany of crime. There was Dr Palmer of Rugely, almost the most horrible and hypocritical of wife poisoners; there was Dr Pritchard, no less hypocritical, who kissed his murdered wife in her coffin, with tears rolling down his cheeks. That frightful creature, Dr Neill Cream, seemed to have given his poisoned pills only to ladies of easy virtue; and such were the victims of Jack the Ripper, probably an accomplished surgeon. Dr George Lamson, son of a clergyman, kept his murder within the family, but the victim of his particularly callous crime was a crippled young brother-in-law. 'Here, Percy, you are a champion pill-taker. Take this,' said the murderer. And so they came to the gentle, little, American Roman Catholic dentist, Dr Crippen.

'That horror!' exclaimed Eliza.

'I'm not sure that he was,' said Philip. 'His wife was a

horrible woman who took drugs. His defence was that he found her dead, and was frightened, and filleted her.'

'What dreadful things doctors can do!'

'Yes, but he was silly. If an intending murderer asked my advice – and he couldn't – I'd say: "Whatever you do, don't cut up the body. Nothing would so set an English jury against you." It's quite illogical, of course.'

'You two have made a fearful story out of poor Mary!' said Eliza.

'Well, if she did murder her husband, she'd be the first English woman doctor to be accused of it,' said Philip. 'But that doesn't make me want to be the victim.'

'One wouldn't like her to go into the Chamber of Horrors with the name of Mary Milsom or Mary Keyworth,' said Jane.

'I've a terrible feeling she might get away with it,' said Philip.

'That would be worse than anything,' said Jane. 'And then the way they try not to hang women, so insulting to our sex, as if we weren't responsible for our actions.'

'Well,' said Eliza when Philip had gone, 'I think we must give up the idea of Mary for him. Behind all that nonsense you could see he was serious about not wanting to have much to do with her.'

'I suppose so,' said Jane regretfully. 'But I should like to see him married. He can well afford it, and I don't like his spending all the time with Mr Freeling.'

'Oh, Jane, Mr Freeling is such a nice young man – and I don't hear any more about their plans for leaving the town.'

'No, and that makes me afraid of something else. Suppose Mr Freeling goes over to Rome? Philip is sure to go with him. Mr Freeling is about as High as one can be.'

'Clergymen aren't doing that much at present,' said Eliza. 'There was quite an epidemic of it about ten years ago, with the New Prayer Book, but it seems to have died down. I shouldn't worry just now.'

'What have you been up to today?' asked James.

'Cooking Mary's goose for her, good and proper.'

'A suitable Christmastide occupation. I hope you weren't too uncharitable?'

'No, I think I did it without an unkind word — rather ingeniously, if I may say so. It had to be done without my telling Aunt Jane that Mary detests her, though I did manage to let Aunt Eliza know — she wasn't in the least surprised.'

'So what did you do?'

'I told Aunt Jane how dangerous it was to marry doctors, as they can so easily murder their spouses, and we went through a whole litany of criminous physicians — Dr Palmer, Dr Pritchard, Dr Crippen....'

'*Orate pro nobis!*' said James. 'How you both love the murderers of England!'

'They make a useful substitute for mythology, when one is talking to people who haven't had a classical education. They ought to be more used.'

'By the way, what do you make of this?' said James. He handed Philip a card, on which Mrs Norman Keyworth invited him to a party in honour of her son Derek's engagement. *Dancing* was printed in the corner.

'It came by the afternoon post, I suppose,' said Philip. 'No doubt I have one too. I imagine we owe these to Doctor Mary. I hardly know how otherwise the second — or is she the third? — Mrs Norman Keyworth could venture to invite you.'

'What course shall we take?'

'You could "plead your clergy", as they used to say. It's rather Low Church for clergymen to dance, isn't it?'

'But I could always go to the card-room, like Jane Austen's clergy, couldn't I?'

'Tut!' said Philip. 'You must refresh your memory of Jane Austen. Father Henry Tilney met Catherine at a ball in Bath, Father Philip Elton is severely rebuked for not dancing with poor Harriet Smith, and Father Collins planned to dance with all the five Miss Bennets in turn at the Netherfield ball.'

'We could find Madingfold too far. It is, isn't it?'

'Yes, and I wish it were further. But I'm afraid Doctor Mary will offer us a lift.'

'You can hardly be in deep enough mourning, I suppose?'

'No, we'll invent "an important parish occasion" in which you need my help,' said Philip. 'After all, we are to address our excuses to "Uncle Norman" and "Aunt What's-her-name", and there's not the slightest need for them to be believed. I would just as soon Doctor Mary disbelieved them.'

13

Sure as fate, Doctor Mary rang up to offer them a lift. 'We can all squeeze into my little car,' she said. 'Would James care to come?'

'Thank you very much,' said Philip. 'But we shan't be going, either of us.'

'Why not?'

'Because we don't want to. Oh, of course we're sending proper excuses to "Uncle Norman" and "Aunt What's-her-name".'

'Dawn.'

'What a name! But I shan't bother you by repeating the same lies.'

'Then I'm not sure that I shall trouble to go myself,' said Mary, almost audibly pouting.

'I shouldn't,' said Philip kindly. 'You'll be warmer at home.'

'You ought to go,' said Mary fussily. 'You ought to go out more and meet people. Good for you and for your practice.'

'My dear Mary,' said Philip in his most superior voice, though the telephone was not his favourite medium, 'Milsom and Dolmidge is an old and reputable firm. We don't go touting for clients, they come to us.... Silly woman!' he said to James. 'She sounds as if I were doing her out of a party. After all, they're her relations not mine.'

'And if she drove us there, who would drive us back?' said James. 'I suppose she meant to stay there.'

'I can't make her out,' said Philip. 'I suppose she only does it to annoy, because she knows it teases.'

'Your Aunt Jane would say it was her odd, awkward way of showing her devotion.'

'She's probably just in need of a partner,' said Philip. 'If I hear any more nonsense about her devotion, I shall begin to think you want to get rid of me. I shall suspect you of making up fairy stories of my devotion to Mary, and feeding her with them. I may not be an old bird, but I'm too old a bird to be caught by Beatrice and Benedict chaff.'

'No one's likely to try it,' said James. 'One doesn't need to be a weather prophet to foresee a violent storm between those two women.'

'Yes, the Mary problem is solved. Or rather we see it now in its original form – Aunt Jane versus the Keyworth family.'

'And you for your Aunt Jane, right or wrong?'

'Of course, but with the hope of protecting Uncle George as far as possible.'

Time went by towards Christmas, and naturally some essential person was ill, and Philip's help was needed on a parish occasion. Excuses are apt to come true, and only the most foolhardy will say 'I shall be ill on such a day', for they will be ill, and they will have brought it on themselves. However, as usual, a number of clerical dons and schoolmasters were spending their holidays in the town. Several of them were glad to help at St Simon's and to participate in a ritual more attractive than that of their school or college chapels. It was therefore quite easy for James to visit his parents on Christmas Day. Philip, who had luncheon with his aunts, was able to give them a vague promise of James at the New Year.

'That will be very nice,' said Jane. 'But one would rather you brought a future wife to introduce to us.'

'*I* wouldn't,' said George. 'I would far rather meet James Freeling than an unknown.'

'Well, if and when I get to know the lady, you shall meet her,' said Philip.

'I don't know how you'll get to know anyone,' said Jane. 'You don't go anywhere. You didn't go to Madingfold.'

'Well, you didn't either, and I'm sure you and Uncle George must have been invited, as it was for Derek's engagement. He's not *my* nephew.'

'I'm too old for parties,' said George. 'And transport is a

problem. Miss Twistleton is out of the way at present. She has just lost her mother.'

'You really ought to get a car,' said Eliza to Philip.

'That's a very sensible suggestion,' said Philip. 'I'd much rather acquire a motor car than a wife – much more use to me, and I couldn't afford both.'

'I'm sure you could.'

'But I don't really think I could manage either,' said Philip. 'And as I don't want to have any children of my own, or to kill other people's, I'll do without both.'

'How absurd you are!' said Eliza.

'I don't generally need a car, Shanks's pony will do for me,' said Philip. 'But I shall want to go over to see you, Uncle George, when you're in the forest.'

'I think you can get the local train to stop at the halt,' said George. 'That's very near.'

'Do you think Danny will consent to come with me?'

'Better leave him to go with your aunt when she takes a car to go over. Anyway, I shall hardly go before New Year's Day.'

Jane and Philip went out for a little walk to digest the Christmas fare and for the sake of Danny – a dreary, grey, Christmas afternoon pottering, one of the most dismal outings of the year.

'You're not spending the evening alone, I hope?' said Jane. 'With your friend away in London.'

'No, we're giving Miss Snape a holiday,' said Philip. 'An old friend is coming round with a car to take me out.'

'You ought to have a house of your own.'

'The third suggestion today of what I ought to have! But at present James and I are quite comfortable where we are. We both have to go out a great deal for our work, and it's convenient to have everything done for us.'

'You can't go on like that for ever.'

'Nothing is for ever,' said Philip. 'But I hope it may be for a long time. We've both got work of our own to do at home, apart from our professional work outside. It's a great thing to have an easy and uncomplicated background.'

'Oh, no doubt it's easy,' said Jane. 'It's easy to be lazy and avoid responsibilities.'

'We're very far from lazy,' said Philip. 'But we save our energies for worthwhile work – James's thesis and my drawing. And our professional work gives us quite enough responsibility.'

'I wonder if other people think as highly of your lives as you do.'

'They wouldn't think about us much,' said Philip. 'In any case, it doesn't much matter what they think now. Work like ours has to be judged by results.'

'And when are we to see these results?'

'I've no idea,' said Philip. 'But we mustn't be hurried. Perhaps there won't be any results.'

'And what then?'

'It will be no one's affair but ours,' said Philip sternly. 'We're trying honestly to use such talents as we have. We're not responsible to anyone on earth.'

'Sometimes I think you're too easily satisfied.'

'I don't like dissatisfied people.'

'But you seem to lack ambition. What do you want out of life?'

'An unworried, quiet life, a few people I'm fond of, time to read and draw...'

'I don't know what your father would have thought.'

'And I don't care, but I don't think Father had as much as I have.'

'He had your mother,' said Jane.

'Not for very long. And afterwards he was no better for it.'

'And he had you.'

'I was nothing to him,' said Philip. 'He tried to do his duty, but fatherhood was of no real interest to him. I could never care for him as I care for Uncle George.'

Jane was rather taken aback and, finding nothing to say, she began looking to see if Danny had done 'his business', the real object of their walk.

'I wish people would leave James and me alone,' said Philip. 'We never interfere with them.'

'I don't suppose you're interested enough in anyone but yourselves.'

'Why should we interest ourselves in other people's affairs unless they ask us to?' said Philip. 'My clients do, and so do James's parishioners – then we have to. But on our own we're contented and do no one any harm. We only ask to be left alone. It's not much to ask.'

'But you might do better with yourselves…'

'*Le mieux est l'ennemi du bien,*' said Philip.

'Oh, it's no good talking to you!' said Jane impatiently, but with no real wish to put an end to the dialogue.

'None at all,' said Philip, 'about some things'; and she was crossly silent.

When they got home they found Eliza strangely disturbed. She had begun to tidy out the long-disused bottom drawers of an old desk, in preparation for moving it, for she was determined to secure the present morning-room for George. Here she had made an unexpected discovery.

'Odd job to do on Christmas Day!' said Jane, in a fault-finding tone.

'The better the day, the better the deed,' said Eliza. She had come upon a pile of old letters tied up with tape; a black-edged envelope at the top was addressed in a scholarly hand to 'Edward Elwell, Esquire'. How could they have got there?

'I think you must have brought back some of poor Ned's papers from Jersey,' said George. 'I know you told me you had destroyed most of them. I suppose you put these aside to go through at home. You had to come back quickly on your mother's account.'

'They look untouched,' said Eliza. 'And I have no recollection of them.'

'Very odd! You who were so attached to Ned,' said Jane unkindly. 'Extraordinary to let them lie forgotten for twenty-five years.'

'Not at all,' said George. 'Eliza was very ill when she got back from Jersey. She'd had a bad shock. Very natural for her to forget them. She wouldn't want to be thinking of such things.'

'And if the letters could be there one year, the other twenty-four would follow as a matter of course,' said Philip.

'That's how it must have been,' said Eliza gratefully. 'And now I really don't know what I ought to do about them.'

'How stupid you are!' said Jane. 'Of course you must read them, and then you'll know.'

'I'm not at all sure that you should,' said George. 'Letters that have lain tied up for twenty-five years can't be in need of an answer. They've answered themselves, if poor Ned never answered them.'

95

'But Ned seems to have tied them up and kept them carefully,' said Jane. 'He evidently attached some importance to them. I'm sure he'd want us to read them.'

'I'm not sure at all,' said Eliza. 'I don't like to poke my nose into a dead man's secrets.'

'Not if he was your brother?'

'Especially as he was my brother,' said Eliza. 'We were very close, but he had his own life. What he didn't tell me, I never wished to know.'

'How well I understand!' said Philip. 'One is full of curiosity about acquaintances, but it is quite different with people one really cares for. One is full of sympathy and interest ready for anything they like to tell us, but one doesn't want to know anything they would like to keep from us.'

'How right you are,' said George. 'I wish everyone felt like that!'

'They're probably of no interest,' said Eliza in a tone that showed she did not believe what she was saying.

'They must have interested Ned,' said Jane. 'So they ought to interest us!'

'I think it dangerous to look into old letters,' said George. 'Sometimes one finds out things one would rather not know. Wiser not to keep letters, and to destroy any one comes across unread.'

'Very cowardly,' said Jane.

'Not really, Aunt Jane,' said Philip. 'You see, there's such a danger of misunderstanding. Unfortunately we can't ask Uncle Ned to explain anything that puzzles us or distresses us. We may know less of the truth, not more, if we read these letters.'

'You think I ought to destroy them?' asked Eliza.

'I certainly do,' said Philip.

'Some people would say we ought to try to get in touch with Ned first,' said Jane.

'Wicked nonsense!' said Eliza. 'How can you think of such a thing?'

'And how do you know they're not quite valuable?' said Jane. 'Ned knew some quite interesting people. We don't know who the letters are from. They may be from someone people want to know about.'

'Then want must be their master,' said Philip. 'I don't care about posterity. Anyway, in the course of history so many important documents have been destroyed that a few more won't matter. It's not at all likely that they're from Bernard Shaw, for instance.'

'If we destroy them, we shall never know,' said Jane.

'Just as well. Aunt Eliza, I beg you to destroy them,' said Philip earnestly.

'I second that,' said George.

'Then I shall,' said Eliza, and threw one into the fire. One could just read 'Dearest Ned' as it burned.

Philip managed to be alone a moment with George.

'Thank goodness we pulled it off,' said his uncle. 'Your Aunt Jane would have liked them to be read aloud. I have a feeling that they weren't for public reading in the family circle.'

'I'm afraid we haven't heard the last of them.'

'No, but as they're gone it doesn't matter,' said George. 'Your Aunt Jane is fond of claiming proprietorship over the dead, and making out that only she cared for them. According to her, the rest of us are quite callous – especially your Aunt Eliza – and we have even hastened their deaths in one way or another.'

'Yes,' said Philip. 'Aunt Eliza took my mother for too long a walk, didn't she? But I can't see how Uncle Ned's death can be laid at her door.'

'No one felt it as she did,' said George.

'Unless, perhaps, the unknown correspondent.'

Later Eliza confided to George: 'Philip looked the image of Ned today, and spoke in his voice. I knew I had to do as he said, and burn the letters.'

'I am sure you were right,' he answered.

'And your Aunt Eliza is not a fanciful woman,' said George, when he communicated this to Philip.

Philip realized that he was now the dearest person on earth to his aunts, not only for his own sake but because he represented to them the people they had most loved in the past. To Eliza he was the image of her young brother Ned, to whom she had been a second mother, and probably more indulgent than the first. To Jane he was the son of her much loved sister Fanny – and Fanny and Ned, the two youngest in the family, had been closely allied and were much alike. He felt thankful to have been able to protect Ned's secrets.

What did he represent to George? He was the son of Fanny, a dear friend and sister, who trusted him as neither of her sisters did. Philip remembered how, during her last illness, she had said: 'George, I'm going to die.' Was it wrong of her to say this in front of him (he was only five)? Or was it a deliberate warning? She had made George her executor. But this was not all. Philip stood to his uncle as a reminder of his own early self – the child who had given him 'quite extraordinary happiness'. He must certainly see that George's interests were protected as far as they lay in his power.

14

Meanwhile time passed. The two sisters decided that they also must go away while the rooms were being decorated, and after long discussion they fixed on Mentone. Miss Twistleton, now a rather tight black bundle, resumed her task; she was probably under the illusion that mourning became her. Eliza and Jane, thinking it would be an affectation to mourn for Rosa for more than three weeks, had gone back to colours, though mourning became them very well. A highly respectable woman was found to act as caretaker while 'the men' were in the house. The maids were sent home, the silver was sent to the bank, and poor little Danny was taken to the excellent woman where he was boarded out. 'Like taking a child to school,' said Jane sentimentally. She had never been to school and did not know how much more agreeable a dog's life could be than that of a small boy.

She began to worry about the safety of their journey; suppose a European war broke out?

'They don't at this time of the year,' said Philip. 'Don't worry.'

'Almost better if it did,' said Jane. 'The horrible injustices that there are in the world, the dreadful things that have happened...'

'No, and no!' said Philip. 'A war never puts right any injustice. If anything is wrong, it makes it worse.'

'But some people want vengeance,' said Jane.

'A wicked thing to want,' said Philip. 'Please God, they will never get it.'

'There's such a thing as righteous indignation,' said Jane.

'I don't think there is,' said Philip. 'It's a name people like to give to their own feelings. I don't believe in "righteousness".'

'You're as bad as your Aunt Eliza and old Kate. You don't worry about all the awful things going on in the world.'

'I wish I didn't,' said Philip. 'I try not to. Worry never did any good. Aunt Eliza and old Kate are quite right. Why be unhappy about what you can't help?'

'But one ought to sympathize. How can one forget those poor Czechs?'

'Easily, I should think. One never gave them a thought before last year. But if they're on your mind you could pray for them, or send a subscription. That's action. Otherwise what's the use of sympathy? It only makes one unhappy, and perhaps disagreeable to one's near neighbours who are in no way to blame, and who have the first claim on one.'

'Who is my neighbour?'

'Aunt Eliza, to begin with, and old Kate.'

'One would think you cared nothing about suffering.'

'An odd conclusion,' said Philip. 'In fact I see a certain amount, living in James's parish. And one of my clients has shown me something of refugee work.'

'I often think too much is done for refugees!' said Jane impatiently. 'I remember how ungrateful the Belgians were during the war, and so tiresome – always wanting butter and cream to cook their vegetables. And I'm told Father Penfold was always having to complain about how badly those Spanish boys behaved at St Philomena's.'

'Yes, I've heard so.'

'And they're big boys of military age,' said Jane. 'Why weren't they in Spain fighting for their country?'

'What is their country? It was a civil war, and they would only have been fighting other Spaniards. Surely it was better to keep them out of it?'

'And the Jews. Of course they've had a dreadful time, but do you really like them?'

'Many of them, very much,' said Philip. 'Clever friends at school and at Oxford. Of course, having a bad time doesn't make people any nicer. My own friends have always been perfectly comfortable.'

'At one time people didn't care much about knowing them,' said Jane. She suddenly laughed. 'Your Aunt Eliza wouldn't like me to tell you this story,' she said, 'but she was a little girl at the time. We were at a garden party of your Great-Aunt

100

Sibylla's, and your Aunt Eliza suddenly recited a dreadful vulgar rhyme she'd picked up from a temporary nursemaid:

> Take a bit of pork
> And put it on a fork
> And give it to a Jew-boy, do!

'Aunt Sibylla had a very distinguished Jewess, a cellist I think, staying with her. She was furious.'

'How embarrassing,' said Philip, laughing. 'But how marvellously unlike Aunt Eliza!'

'She was seven or thereabouts. Luckily for her Aunt Sibylla – ridiculous woman – thought your grandmother had put her up to it, and said so. Your grandmother was so angry that your Aunt Eliza got off without a scolding.'

'I'm glad of that. Children's feelings are so hurt by injustice. It would have been enough to make her anti-Jewish for life. I hope she's completely forgotten it.'

Dilatoriness on the part of the decorators and severe weather delayed Jane and Eliza's journey. Jane was so much afraid of the Channel crossing that she lay awake at nights listening to every wind, like the sailor's mother in the ballads. She began to feel seasick on leaving the house.

'I thought they'd never get off,' said Philip, 'but Aunt Eliza by herself would be quite a good traveller.'

'I'm sure she never fusses about being on time,' said James, 'and never misses a train.'

'Exactly, but Aunt Jane never takes her eye off the clock. She repeats: "Better an hour too soon than a minute too late."'

'I hope she doesn't apply that precept to her social engagements?'

'No, but she is dreadfully punctual if she goes to the theatre. And she complicates their route, because she's afraid of going through London or Paris. Indeed, as she says, "one takes one's life in one's hands" if one gets into a Paris taxi.'

'I'm told that in every pair of people living together, married or not, there are never two train fuss-pots,' said James, thereby revealing where he stood.

'Yes, I know I'm like Aunt Jane,' said Philip. 'And I shall probably grow more like her as I get older. But in one thing I'm more like Aunt Eliza. She has her nose in her novel all the time, while Aunt Jane looks out of the window or observes the people in the carriage.'

'What will her novel be?'

'It will probably be French, to "rub up her French",' said Philip. 'Perhaps she is rereading *Le roman d'un jeune homme pauvre,* or she's got a French translation of some English novel, because French books may be "beastly".'

'How good is their French?'

'Not at all good. When they were young they were sent to Dresden for German. They lived in the English chaplain's family, and had to drink table beer because the water was so bad. They hated it. The clergyman's little son was so thirsty in hot weather that he got drunk, and fell off his chair.'

'So they didn't do much about French?'

'Oh, I think they went for walks with a "Mademoiselle" when they got home again, but that can't have made much impression. They used to think my father spoke French well, which was far from the case.'

'I think women of that age and class are generally rather insular, unless they become Italianate like Miss Springfield.'

'Who's in hospital, poor thing, with a broken leg,' said Philip. 'So she couldn't get off to Bordighera, or wherever. I must go and see her. My aunts' insularity is largely economic. They're not mean, but they expect foreigners to cheat them. They don't understand the exchange, and imagine that the French can buy much more with their francs than they actually can. And they will sail out of hotels, past people waiting for tips, saying, "We paid ten per cent for service", and they'll expect to be thanked.'

'I dare say they are, ironically.'

'I wouldn't be surprised. Then they are odd about the food – on the whole they enjoy it, but they're morbidly afraid the Frogs will put garlic into everything, even into the *café au lait.*'

Philip threw the local paper across the breakfast table to James. 'Bloody Bayne up to his tricks again,' he said.

'Hum, perhaps,' said James, after reading a letter on the correspondence page. 'Though we don't know if the first precious composition was due to him.'

'I'll look for it, and compare the style,' said Philip. 'I don't remember that it was quite so uneducated.'

Bayne had written to protest against 'Romish practices' at St Simon's. In particular he said he was outraged at the 'children's corner' that had been contrived by James with Philip's assistance. Its blessing had been the 'important parish occasion' offered (though unspecified) as an excuse to Madingfold.

'I've never heard of a Roman church with a children's corner,' said Philip.

'I think it's because it's in the Lady Chapel,' said James. 'It's "the thin end of the wedge towards Mariolatry", as he beautifully expresses himself.'

'A very thin end to a very long wedge.'

'Ah, but "innocent children" are involved!' said James. 'And here's for me: "... the snowy-banded, delicate handed, dilettante priest".'

'That's from Tennyson – *Maud*. You can't sue him for that.'

'What can he mean by "dilettante"?'

'I don't suppose he knows, or that Tennyson knew either.'

'What shall we do about it?'

'Hang up another lamp,' said Philip, 'and put a few more candles and flowers about.'

'I hope the Vicar won't be feeble about this.'

'He hardly can, as he blessed it. By the way, I wish the clergy were a bit more chary about blessing things – all those lethal weapons! Some of them say they'll bless defensive but not offensive weapons.'

'I know. "*Def*ensive, not *off*ensive," they say, which is hypocrisy as well as bad elocution – as if the same weapons couldn't nearly always be used for both purposes.'

'Almost everything, except gas masks.'

'Aunt Eliza really believes our submarines are different from German U-boats and purely defensive – in fact only meant to sink U-boats, which are "devilish". And I asked her what she thought bombing aeroplanes were for, and she said to drop bombs on other aeroplanes – which would be a difficult feat. I dare say she hasn't heard of fighting aeroplanes.'

'Did you disillusion her?'

'I started trying to – one can't help being annoyed when people say such stupid things. But she's so firmly convinced *we* wouldn't do anything "beastly", no matter what the Huns did.'

'Kinder, perhaps, to leave her her illusions,' said James. 'They may be a comfort to her one day. But it is rather desperate to think that she is above the average of education and intelligence among the electorate. How can one believe in democracy?'

'One need only believe other forms of government are worse,' said Philip. 'I suppose it's the way in which some people manage to believe in the English climate.'

'"George Hamilton Bayne",' he repeated, after a pause. 'Shall I tell the aunts about him? I shall be writing tomorrow or the day after.'

'To Mrs Keyworth?'

'Yes. To them both, of course, but addressed to her. She's the better correspondent, and often amusing about the people they meet in hotels.'

'Don't they have the local paper sent on?'

'No. The thing is, whether to remind them of Bayne or not. One wants them to forget the first incident, but it was convenient to use him as a scapegoat then, and one might want him again.'

'I'm not sure that's fair,' said James.

'It isn't illegal. I only suggested it could have been Bayne, and of course it could. He can't sue me for that.'

'Well, I suppose if you go no further than that, it isn't immoral either.'

'Anyway, I have the right to tell them what's in print, and without comment,' said Philip.

'And how will they react?'

'I'm afraid Aunt Jane may be tempted to think there's something in it, but Aunt Eliza will be able to strike a crushing blow. She'll point out that what goes on at St Simon's is no business of George Hamilton Bayne's because he is a nonconformist – and that, consequently, he is no gentleman.'

15

'Where shall I begin collecting copy for my letter to Mentone?' asked Philip.

'I shouldn't begin it with Bayne,' said James. 'It makes him too important. What about paying a visit to Danny?'

'Won't that be raising his hopes rather cruelly?'

'No, I think he'll be glad to see someone from home,' said James.

'Anyhow, Aunt Jane will want news of him, and I'll put her feelings first. I hope I shall find Mrs Simpson at the piano, and Danny at her heel, in the boom of the tingling strings. He loves her hymn-singing – dogs are so Protestant.'

Danny was as near Mrs Simpson's feet as he could be, allowing for her constant use of the pedals.

'Oh, do go on, please!' said Philip, accepting a dark cup of tea. Danny had received him graciously, and had gone so far as to lick his hand. Now he resumed his place under the piano-stool, and Mrs Simpson resumed her song:

'Hark! hark my soul! Angelic songs are swelling
O'er Earth's green fields and Ocean's wave-beat shore:
How sweet the truth those blessèd strains are telling
Of that new life when sin shall be no more.'

'A lovely hymn,' said Philip. 'Can't we have another?'

'I'm afraid I already hear my cousin at the door. Danny doesn't seem to take to poor Frederic. He's been through cruel sufferings, and now he's in,' – *sotto voce* – a *'home.'* They let him out in the afternoons, and he likes to come here because he knows that I know what he's been through with his wife – a cruel, wicked women. Mr Milsom, as a nurse, I've seen many bad women, but Mrs Frederic Clapp takes, if I may so put it, the cake.'

105

'You'd like me to leave you?'

'Oh, please, Mr Milsom, not yet. Frederic might think you wanted to avoid him. He's so sensitive. And you'll find him a really clever man.'

Danny growled, and a slim, elderly man entered, dressed with an old-fashioned youthful elegance. He wore a rose in his buttonhole.

'Frederic, this is dear Mrs Keyworth's nephew,' said Mrs Simpson. 'You know what a true friend she has been to me in bad times. He has come to see my darling lodger, to send his auntie news of him.'

'A kind, a beautiful thought,' said Frederic Clapp.

'You've had tea, Frederic?'

'No, the Matron would not give it me so early. She flew into a rage when I asked her. She is far more fit to be certified than I am.'

Mrs Simpson rang the bell for 'the girl'.

'The lunatic will now entertain you at the piano,' said Frederic ironically. 'You observe that he is not in a strait waistcoat, as you might expect. The lunatic will sing you a song – words and music are both of his own composition.'

He struck a chord, and lifted up his voice:

'I told my ta-hale to the whispering breeze....'

Danny decided to howl too.

'And this was written by the lunatic, words *and* music.'

'Very talented,' said Philip.

'Do you think your dear aunt would care for me to come and sing in her drawing-room,' said Frederic. 'One afternoon when she is entertaining her friends? I would make no charge.'

'It would make him known to all the first families in the place,' said Mrs Simpson.

'My aunts never have a reception of that sort,' said Philip. 'If I ever hear of anyone who does, I shall not fail to mention you.' Then, with a reassuring touch of Danny's cold nose, he took his leave.

His next objective was Miss Springfield in the orthopaedic hospital. What flowers to take her? Something robust in keeping with her character, and if possible something to

106

remind her of Italy. In the end he bought sprays of mimosa –
not a very good choice, for the fluff goes at once and leaves
you with dry little balls. But the immediate scent and
cheerfulness must give pleasure.

'So you find me still in this vile climate,' said Miss
Springfield.

'I hope they keep your room warm enough?'

'Yes, but one can see how ghastly it must be outside. Lucky
Jane and Eliza at Mentone.'

'Aunt Jane complains of an icy wind.'

'She'll come back to a pretty kettle of fish,' cackled Miss
Springfield. 'Do you know that Twistleton woman has settled
in at the Forest Hotel and is your uncle's constant
companion? What will your Aunt Jane say to that?'

'She will not be pleased,' said Philip. 'But I suppose that will
soon be over. He will be coming home when my aunts come.'

'Don't you be too sure of that. He seems firmly dug in, and
so does she.'

'How do you hear these things, Donna Caterina?'

'Dear boy, by being confined to my room. Everyone is so
kind, and brings me titbits of news. I've heard more in a week
here than I'd hear in a month at home.'

'Yes, when it's an entertainment for the sick, gossip
becomes one of the works of mercy.'

'But I don't want dear Jane to be upset. Do you think she
knows anything about it?'

'I don't think anyone in the place writes to her. She only
writes to relations herself. I'm going to write one of these
days, but I'd rather not mention this.'

'No, much better not.'

'But she'll want me to give her some account of Uncle
George.'

'Well, ring up and invite yourself to luncheon on Sunday,
then he will have warning, and the Twistleton will probably
be sent out of the way.'

'You mustn't talk as if there were "something" between
them.'

'I know there can't be, ha, ha!' chuckled Miss Springfield.
'And evidently you do too. But there's enough appearance of
evil to make tongues wag – and that's what will upset your
aunt.'

'Better to leave it for her when she comes back,' said Philip, 'and not to spoil her holiday.'

'Do you think she'd come rushing back?'

'She'd talk of it, but Aunt Eliza would say: "How stupid you are! The men are still in the house." It's mainly for Aunt Eliza's sake that I'll say nothing – she'd have a very thin time.'

'I'm afraid so. Well, you may send them news of me. I ought to go home next week. I hope you've been to see Danny?'

'He seems very comfortable and happy, and enjoys his landlady's hymn-singing.'

'Jane won't want him to be *too* happy without her.'

'Well, I can tell her that he was unusually gracious to me. He licked my hand.'

'That looks as if he were thinking of home.'

'How's Musso? Does he come to see you?'

'Not allowed, but Florrie brings me news – dear little dog!'

The next objective was the house. Philip arranged to meet Mrs Mullins, the caretaker, there one day after office hours. Of course the work was protracted as 'the men' were paid by the hour, and every two hours Mrs Mullins was expected to bring them tea. The rooms, both unfinished, smelt of paint and cigarette smoke, that abominable mixture that is especially revolting in closed rooms and cold weather. Philip told Mrs Mullins that they must be thoroughly aired and perhaps fumigated before his aunts returned. The rest of the house appeared to be well kept, in spite of the piling up of furniture. He was promised an early date for the end of the decoration, and Mrs Mullins very much wanted to get the men out of the house – then, it appeared, she hoped to hold a seance. Philip was too much taken aback to find words, and after he had left he realized that he ought to have forbidden it. 'But I expect it will come to nothing,' he consoled himself.

There remained only his visit to the Forest Hotel before he could write his letter.

'That will need great care,' said James. 'You must have sympathy for both sides?'

'For my uncle and aunt, yes, but I don't know so much about the Twistleton. I reserve judgement there.'

In the end it was George who took the initiative.

'Your uncle on the phone, Mr Philip,' said Miss Snape, for the first time adopting this form of address. 'I hope there's no bad news of your aunties?'

'Can you come over to luncheon on Sunday?' asked George. 'My niece Mary will motor you over if you can.'

'She seems to be constantly hereabouts,' Philip complained. 'I'm afraid she must be neglecting her work in London.'

'You sound just like your Aunt Jane!' said James,

Mary put up a cheek, which was not kissed. 'Philip dear, how nice to see you after all this time.'

'Has it been more than six weeks?' said Philip. 'That day we went to Crampton?'

Mary pouted.

'Of course there's been Christmas in between, and that slows things up,' said Philip. 'Did you spend it with "Uncle Stanley" and "Aunt Eileen" – and how are they?'

'Don't be nasty,' said Mary. 'No, I took a holiday in Switzerland.'

'You do seem to get about,' said Philip. 'Are you staying at Madingfold now?'

'No, Uncle George invited me for the weekend.'

'And how do you find him?'

'So much better. I should like him to stay there till the weather is warmer, and I dare say he will. Miss Twistleton is able to go on with the good work.'

Was she in residence? Was old Kate's story an exaggeration? What part was Mary playing in all this? He did not feel that he could ask outright.

'Apparently you're not bringing Danny?'

'No dogs allowed in the hotel, thank goodness.'

'Uncle George would have liked to see him more than anyone,' said Philip. 'But Danny seems quite happy with Mrs Simpson. She sings hymns to him, which he loves.'

'To him?'

'Well, to herself, I suppose, and perhaps to the Almighty. But Danny's the only human listener – mortal, I should say.'

'Like you to say "human",' said Mary. 'I think your family prefers dogs to people.'

'I wouldn't quite say that,' said Philip, 'though of course I don't care whether unknown people like me or not. But I always want to be liked by dogs or children.'

'How very odd.'

'Not at all. They're innocent creatures with pure instincts. People aren't. If dogs or children dislike you, there's very likely something wrong with you.'

'But you wouldn't want to live with dogs and children only?'

'No, I want to live with intelligent people – with people whom I can understand and who speak the same language.'

'Do you call your aunts intelligent, then?'

'In their way. Neither of them could read Kant, for instance, nor can I. But Aunt Eliza has a logical mind and Aunt Jane has imagination. Anyhow, as Rousseau or someone like that says, affection nourishes the mind and not only the heart. When you've always loved people they don't bore you, and they understand you.'

'I've not found that.'

'Poor Mary!' said Philip, with real sympathy. 'I'm afraid you haven't had anything like that in your life – not at least since Granny Keyworth died.'

'My dear, I believe you're right,' said Mary, taking a hand off the wheel to grip his arm.

'Pity you don't care for dogs,' said Philip, disengaging himself.

Uncle George offered them sherry, as he could not at home. Otherwise he seemed quite his old self.

'So you went to see Danny, old boy?' he said to Philip. 'How was he? Dear little dog!'

'Happy on the whole, I think,' said Philip. 'But very gracious to me. He licked my hand.'

'Tell your aunt that,' said George. 'He must be homesick.'

'He loved Mrs Simpson's hymns, but he was much displeased when there was a visit from her dotty cousin Frederic Clapp.'

'That scamp!' said George. 'Dogs always know! I'd no idea she was connected with him. She's a decent woman, by all accounts.'

'What's wrong with the man Clapp?'

'Ladies present,' murmured George.

'Uncle George, I'm not a lady, I'm a doctor,' said Mary.

'Indecent exposure,' said George quickly, to get it out. 'Several offences on the heath.'

'Odd I never heard of it,' said Philip.

'You were abroad at the time. He was ordered psychiatric treatment.'

'Well, let's hope he won't do it again,' said Mary.

'He wanted to give a recital in the aunts' drawing-room,' said Philip with a giggle. 'Anyway, he can't sing, so there's no reason to risk it. And Danny won't mind what he does.'

'If he's an exhibitionist, he'll want more of an audience than Danny,' said Mary.

'Well, let's forget about him, shall we?' said George, and he gave a very optimistic account of his health, warmly commending Miss Twistleton's massage. Philip carefully refrained from asking how often this was given, and no more was said about it.

In the dining-room George indicated various elderly gentlemen. There was Admiral This and Colonel That, he said with some satisfaction. Evidently in the years since his retirement he had felt deprived of the society of men of his own age. It was also evident to Philip, who had never had occasion to notice it before, that George felt the inferiority that some businessmen observably and unnecessarily feel when confronted with members of the armed forces, even when the latter are in no way their superiors in class or education. This respect, of course, was limited to the mature, for George had no admiration for the cousins at Comstead.

Philip reported on the alterations in the house.

'Typical of the British working man,' said George. 'Ten minutes off every hour, and nothing done in a fortnight that could be stretched over three weeks.' Otherwise he seemed to feel little interest, and turned the conversation to Philip's work.

'New book, and I've got to find a lot of new models,' he said. 'I want a rather solid little girl, four rather flashy parents, and an elderly, shabby governess with steel spectacles.'

'You'll find that one all right,' said Mary.

111

'She's the easiest, as there's nothing period about her clothes.'

'But four parents seems rather a large allowance.'

'That was the trouble,' said Philip. 'Poor Maisie.'

16

'Mary doesn't know what she's at,' said Philip.

'Probably you don't know that either,' said James.

'It's not specially important to me to know. But she ought to know more about physiology and psychology than I do.'

'One hopes so.'

'Yet she hasn't lost that irritating habit of pawing me as if she wanted sex, and wanted me. She doesn't in the least want either, and she ought to know by now they're incompatible.'

'She may not. And people often want incompatible things. Novels have been written about it.'

'But it's annoying. Of course I think I know what she wants, or rather what would make her happy – an emotional friendship with another woman and a nice cosy male confidant.'

'Just like your aunts, you want to arrange her life for her!'

'Well, I'd do it better than she will,' said Philip, and laughed too.

'You'd do quite well for the male confidant,' said James generously.

'If I liked her better. But, poor thing, I think she needs someone to care about more than someone to care about her.'

'We're being presumptuous in supposing she hasn't got both,' said James. 'I feel sure she has lots of female adorers in the medical world.'

'I hope we can leave her to them for quite a time.'

'Has she really got no family?'

'Only one cousin on the Keyworth side, Derek. Uncle George says he's a "decent chap", so I'm sure he is now, though he was a detestable boy. He's just been married, or is just going to be, to "the Honourable Molly".'

'Who's she?'

'A Wiggins, daughter of a recently ennobled pork butcher. I've never seen her, but I understand she's been to a good school and is quite presentable – at any rate as presentable as she has any need to be.'

'Not even a distant whiff of the unclean animal?'

'So I'm told. I amuse myself thinking what escutcheon I could make for them if I were in the Herald's Office – strings of sausages.'

'They could have a boar's head for a crest, like Ruskin – with a lemon in the mouth for difference.'

'*Mrs Reginald Mullins At Home*. Spooks,' said Philip.

'You're making it up.'

'Yes, or rather abbreviating it. She's not at home, but *chez mes tantes*, and she can't positively promise unearthly visitants. She has the effrontery to invite us to a seance.'

'I shall "plead my clergy",' said James. 'I have no business there.'

'I suppose I oughtn't to go? But I'm a bit curious.'

'I think you might go. Perhaps you ought to hold what I believe in your profession is called "a watching brief" for your aunts.'

'Not exactly, but I see what you mean. I'll go and bow my head in the house of Rimmon, as they say in your profession.'

'You see, she might produce unruly spooks. Poltergeists perhaps.'

'Awful if they began chucking my aunts' china about.'

'I believe the things they throw are said to sail slowly through the air, and not to break – but one wouldn't care to chance it.'

'No, I shouldn't like to see a nice Meissen tureen floating through the air. One wouldn't know whether to try to field it or to leave it to do its will.'

'It was awful,' said Philip afterwards. 'I oughtn't to have gone.'

'I'm sorry I encouraged you.'

'Dear James, it was all my own fault. You were indulging my curiosity, that was all. Well, "Curiosity killed the cat."'

114

'And lost us Paradise, for that matter. But I was curious too.'

'I see I was stupidly afraid of snubbing Mrs Mullins, and seeming snobbish – there are many much worse faults. I ought to have replied: "Mr Philip Milsom is surprised at being invited to a reception in his aunts' house during their absence, and for a purpose of which they would not approve." It is so obvious now. I felt inhibited because I had made no objection when she first spoke of it.'

'You were taken by surprise then, as well you might have been.'

'But other people seem to have judged rightly. Naturally there were no "nice" people there – with one exception. I don't know if she had ventured to ask any. Of course they couldn't accept her invitation to my aunts' house.'

'Yes, we were foolish,' said James. 'However, there can't be any sequel. Who was the one "nice" person?'

'Poor Mrs Dolmidge, my partner's wife. I told her I was watching things for my aunts' sake.'

'True enough, if a poor excuse. But it was for her to feel embarrassed at meeting you there. Why had she come?'

'Poor soul, she lost a young son years ago – meningitis – and she seizes on every opportunity of communicating with the other world. Oh, James, it's so cruel to practise on people like that!'

'Was the medium obviously a fraud?'

'I don't know. Perhaps she wasn't consciously. She sat in a corner of the drawing-room in that rather ugly Victorian chair we call "Aunt Sibylla's chair". She looked rather fuddled. And at the piano, who but Mrs Simpson!'

'Not Danny?'

'No, "I've not brought my sweet lodger. He wouldn't like to come home and not find his mistress. Besides, dogs are so psychic." I do think they have a nose for evil – Danny would have howled. But she'd brought the egregious Frederic Clapp.'

'Then hymns, I suppose,' said James. 'If I'd been there they would have asked me to open the proceedings with a prayer.'

'"Prevent us O Lord in all our doings,"' said Philip. 'As it was, we had "Jerusalem the Golden" enlivened by the rich baritone of Clapp. In that company it sounded appallingly vulgar:

'The shout of them that triumph
The song of them that feast.

'It made me imagine a sort of Baptist beano or school treat
in a temperance hotel, with bottles of orange squash and
tomato ketchup on the table.'

'So far, you've told me nothing for Danny to object to,' said
James. 'Dogs rather like vulgarity – though they ought to be
aristocrats, with their splendid pedigrees.'

'Yes, but that horrible woman in Aunt Sibylla's chair! Will
you exorcize it for me, James?'

'I don't think it's necessary. Put it in the sun, when there is
any.'

'It was obvious that she couldn't be in communication with
Holy Souls,' said Philip. 'But she might easily be in touch with
the Bottomless Pit. So very disgusting to have her there in my
aunts' house, putting it in direct contact with hell.'

'But we all are, all the time,' said James. 'Each of us has an
ever open telephone line to heaven and hell.'

'Well, the lights were put out or lowered, and there was
uneasy silence for a time. Then the control – or whatever you
call it – came on. She was a Fräulein Schechner, a German
governess who had lived in an English family some eighty
years ago.'

'Better than a Red Indian guide. The usual nonsense, I
suppose?'

'Yes – at least I suppose it is usual. Some of the dim little
people sitting round got messages of a vague kind. "Vey so
vonderfully happy are", or "Vey pick *Blumen* – how you say,
blossoms?"'

'That's harmless enough. Silly rather than evil.'

'But I had a nasty shock. It appeared that there was a
special message for me. It was from someone who had once
lived in the house. I wasn't exactly named, and most people
might not have realized it. I might ask questions mentally, and
the spirit would answer "yes" or "no".'

'Uncle Ned?'

'That's what I thought, or perhaps my mother. I made my
mind a blank as far as I could, and said silently *Vade me retro
Satana.*'

'And there was a reply: "Yes"?'

'You've guessed right.'

'And poor Mrs Dolmidge?'

'She had to go empty away. But I think she's used to it.'

'Better so.'

'Do you think the medium or Mrs Mullins had done some research,' said Philip.

'The Devil could have told them,' said James. 'Lies, perhaps, but something to go on.'

'Then the lights came on, and Clapp had his great moment.'

'Not...?' began James.

'Patience, or you'll spoil the story. Mrs Simpson said: "What's the time, Frederic?" Clapp turned towards the middle of the room, smiled all round, opened the fastener of his trousers, put in a hand and pulled out...'

'Not...?' cried James.

'No – how quick the clergy are to think evil! – I must disappoint you. He pulled out a gold watch at the end of a long chain.'

'Sensation!'

'Not quite as much as I dare say he hoped. I'm not sure that anyone except myself expected something *worse*. But I immediately asked Mrs Simpson for another hymn, so as to have a moment to regain my gravity.'

'And she gave you "Peace Perfect Peace"?'

'You're a wizard, James. Of course she did. Then Mrs Dolmidge gave me a lift home – her chauffeur was waiting. She was nice – pathetic but dignified about poor Christopher.'

'I suppose you knew him well, and couldn't feel the same way at all?'

'Of course I wasn't his mother, but that's not what you mean. I disliked him very much if we met at parties. You know, the neat sort of boy, with the tie-pin always in place, and greased hair with an immaculate parting. But he went to some other school – Oliver's school, I can't remember which it was, can you? Anyway, he was a nice-looking boy, and Oliver was devoted to him.'

'He would be,' said James with a smile.

'How quick the clergy are to think evil, as I see you do! But do you know – no, that's a silly rhetorical question because

117

you can't possibly, and I didn't know myself till less than an hour ago – Oliver still keeps up with Mrs Dolmidge? He even visits her when he's this way – busy as he probably is with Larborough and Ribbentrop.'

'That's very nice of him, and I own I should never have expected it.'

'No, you wouldn't!' said Philip teasingly. 'And you see he kept his good deeds hidden from us.'

'I dare say he was ashamed. He might think he was being rather sentimental,' said James.

'And is that "thinking the best of people"?' asked Philip with a smile. 'I admit I have always kept poor Mrs D at a distance. As a motherless boy I might have been a godsend to a bereaved mother. But I hadn't liked Christopher at all, and I didn't in the least want her to be a mother to me.'

'I should think not. Your aunts wouldn't have liked that a bit.'

'Well, now I must compose a letter of apology to Aunt Eliza. I must get in before anyone else tells them about the seance, though I don't know who could except Mrs Simpson.'

'Your Aunt Eliza?'

'Yes. She'll mind about it more – and any excuse addressed to her must hold water, she has the more logical mind. Aunt Jane might almost be tempted to think there was something in all that nonsense. Anyway, I wrote to her just the other day.'

'You won't wait a day for the local paper? There may be more of Bayne and his antics.'

'I think not. I want to get my letter off as soon as possible. And I rather feel mention of anything else might be shabby – almost as if it were to distract attention from my foolishness.'

'I quite envy Canon Robson,' said James. 'You must be the best sort of penitent. "Bless me, Father" ... and then you come straight out with your worst sin.'

'Cowardice, don't you think, to get the worst out first?'

'It's not how cowardly people behave,' said James.

My dear Aunt Eliza (wrote Philip),

A very disagreeable thing has happened, but I don't think it can have any consequences. I am very sorry I did not prevent it, but I am not sure if this was possible. When I visited the house ten days ago, Mrs Mullins talked of holding a seance. I didn't take this seriously, or I would have wired to you. To my horror, two days ago I received an invitation to one in your drawing-room. I didn't feel I had the authority to forbid it, and did not quite like to bring in Uncle George. I see that I ought simply to have replied that I couldn't accept invitations from anyone else to your house, though I doubt if that would have made her call it off. Instead I stupidly went; not, of course, to take any part in that wicked nonsense, but just to keep an eye on things – and though it was horrible and vulgar (and so were the people there), it wasn't unseemly in any way. Before leaving I told Mrs Mullins that I was surprised that she should hold such a meeting in your house, and asked her if she had your permission. Of course she had nothing to say to that.

'You didn't tell me that,' said James. 'It seems you have quite justified yourself. And it was kinder to your aunt not to mention Ned, and kinder to Mrs Dolmidge not to betray her.'

'I'm afraid Aunt Jane might have said: "But perhaps Ned really had something to say to you."'

17

Philip was again invited to the Forest Hotel, and this time it was Miss Twistleton who came to fetch him. 'I'm so glad of this chance to talk to you,' she said. 'I know how much Mr Keyworth owes to your sympathy and understanding.'

An ominous opening. Evidently more sympathy and understanding were going to be asked for, and might be more difficult to produce.

'He would have had a sad time in that house without you,' she went on.

'You must forgive me,' said Philip, anxious to atone for his lapse about the seance by scrupulous loyalty. 'I don't feel that I can discuss my aunts.'

'Oh, Mr Philip!' cried Miss Twistleton. 'You can't have thought I wished to criticize your aunts! Oh, what a dreadful idea!'

'No, of course you wouldn't,' said Philip soothingly.

'No, what a dreadful idea!' said Miss Twistleton. 'I meant it was a great thing for him to have another man about.'

'Yes, since his retirement he hasn't seen much of other men,' said Philip. 'He has no club here, and no cronies. He only came back from the office to sleep here, sometimes at home and sometimes at his mother's.'

'Oh, you *do* understand!' said Miss Twistleton. 'How dreadful if you had thought I was going to criticize your aunts!'

'Of course you wouldn't,' said Philip in a final tone, and as much as to say 'You'd better not!' 'It's rather a pity he never played golf – even now on a good day he could get round a course. And he's never been a bridge player. I hate cards myself, but I see what people mean when they say I'm preparing for a sad old age.'

'He isn't really close to his own family,' said Miss Twistleton, almost as if making atonement for a supposed slight to Philip's. 'Though dear Doctor Mary is trying to do her best.'

'It is to her that we owe you,' said Philip, as a sort of honourable amend.

'You are very kind to say so,' she said. 'I do think I have managed to help him a bit. He walks much more easily now. But the great thing is that he is more cheerful out here. After all, he's a real countryman. He's enjoying the forest, and he has taken up his drawing again.'

'I'm delighted to hear it. It was a great sacrifice for him to become a businessman instead of being a countryman and an artist,' said Philip. 'That was his father's doing,' he was careful to add.

'Well, now one would like him to get some good out of his retirement,' said Miss Twistleton, 'to make up for some of that wasted time.'

'It's a bit difficult. He's rather set in his ways.'

'That's where a new broom like Doctor Mary could sweep the cobwebs away. Naturally you, Mr Philip, have thought of him as quite settled down – and your kindness has meant a lot to him. But Doctor Mary decided he needed rousing. I hope you don't mind my saying this?'

'No, but I hope he doesn't mind being "roused", as you call it. People very often do.'

'It's for his own good.'

'My dear Miss Twistleton, I have suffered a great deal more from things done for my own good than from anything done to me out of malice.'

She drove on in silence for a while.

'It's a great thing to be able to talk to you,' she then remarked. 'You fully understand your uncle's difficulties – also you represent his present home, and its claims.'

'His present home!' exclaimed Philip. 'I hope you are not suggesting that he is going to leave it?'

'Oh no,' she said, rather awkwardly. 'I only meant he might prolong his stay in the forest for a while, and perhaps make a habit of going back there from time to time for a sort of rest-cure.'

'It might not be at all a bad idea,' said Philip cautiously.

'Then my aunts could get away more often if they wanted to. They used to, when old Mrs Keyworth was alive.'

There was another silence.

'My aunts have been at a good deal of trouble to make the house more comfortable for him,' Philip observed. 'I hope he'll come home for a time soon after they return.'

'Oh, I'm sure,' said Miss Twistleton vaguely.

There was silence again, and Philip uneasily reflected on the difficulties in front of him. He must not allow any criticism of his aunts except from George himself; and yet he must not interfere with George's struggle for freedom and perhaps for life. After all, Jane did not really much want him back, except as a matter of sentiment, and to save face; while Eliza would be glad to have him frequently out of the house. This, however, must not be admitted in front of Miss Twistleton or Mary. Yet George must not be discouraged; if he had any duties to Jane or Eliza he was quite capable of seeing them for himself. Luckily money in no way entered into the affair: Jane and Eliza were quite independent of George's contribution to the household, and there was no reason to think he would not still play his part.

'Will Mary Keyworth be there today?' he asked.

'She promised to try to get over,' said Miss Twistleton. 'She particularly wants to talk to you.'

Philip's heart sank yet further.

And there she was in the hall. 'Hilda, your patient is waiting for you,' she said. 'I'll take a little stroll in the garden with my cousin before lunch.'

So that was how it was to be; perhaps better so.

'Philip, we've arrived at a critical point,' she began. 'Uncle George, as you'll see for yourself, is another man. He stands upright, walks quite easily, takes an interest in everything – not just in his own aches and pains. He has a cheerful room, and not one medicine bottle in it. Hilda Twistleton has been quite wonderful with him.'

'Does she come over often to give him massage?'

'She has a room here, and gives him massage every day,' said Mary. 'She has other patients in the hotel, so it suits her very well – and her home is broken up now her old mother is dead.'

'Ah, yes,' said Philip, non-committally.

122

'She acts as a chauffeur too, and drives Uncle George about. You know how he loves the forest.'

'Yes, indeed.'

'Well, the question is, is this to continue, or is Uncle George to go back to that dreary half-life?'

'I suppose it's for him to answer that.'

'If he's allowed to,' said Mary. 'Philip, you're not holding a brief for your aunt, as I think they say in your profession?'

'I'm a solicitor. I don't hold briefs.'

'Oh, you know what I mean!' said Mary impatiently.

'Perhaps as well as you do,' said Philip. 'I don't want to discuss Aunt Jane.'

'I respect that,' said Mary insincerely. 'But you'll agree that their marriage has come to an end?'

'It depends on what you mean. Marriage is supposed to be for life, isn't it?'

'Oh, I dare say,' said Mary. 'Of course you're churchy, but you'll admit that people can separate and live better apart sometimes? This marriage is no longer a living thing in any sense.'

'You may be right,' said Philip, 'but I never think other people can judge. One doesn't know what it's like to be married – and please God, one never will. There must be a kind of surrender of one's individuality that we can't imagine. And something must remain after thirty years.'

'Precious little, in some cases.'

'More, I think, in that generation than in our own,' said Philip. 'My only feeling is that I don't want to interfere.'

'Well, we can rely on your neutrality?'

'As far as I can foresee.'

Then Mary went on to propose a startling development. The hotel was all very well, but it was rather expensive for two people. Uncle George was very much better, but he really preferred to have his breakfast in bed; and in cold wet weather he might occasionally like to spend a whole day there. The hotel people were not very agreeable about sending up trays; they insisted that it was a hotel and not a nursing home. . . .

'It will be easier for him to have trays at home now,' said Philip. 'His room is changed to downstairs. And Miss

123

Twistleton can come over for his massage whenever he likes. I suppose she'll go on living in the town?'

But Mary had another plan. There was a small gardener's cottage to let on the hotel estate; it was particularly well equipped and furnished, since sometimes it had been used as an annexe to the hotel. George could be settled in it, with an old servant of his mother's to cook for him. Miss Twistleton would continue her good work, and he could enjoy such society as the hotel had to offer. Besides, he would have a little garden of his own in which he would like to potter about.

'It might do as a *pied-à-terre*,' said Philip, 'when he wants a short change from home. You know he used to have a small cottage on Dartmoor for holidays.'

'It might *be* home,' said Mary.

'I don't imagine he quite wants that,' said Philip coldly. 'And I can't imagine my aunt's reactions being very favourable. I'm not here to answer for her, but I will venture to ask you a small favour which I'd rather not speak of to Uncle George.'

'Yes?'

'If there's any lease or contract, I'd rather my firm wasn't brought into it. We're my aunt's solicitors, after all.'

'That's fair enough.'

'Not that I like to oblige anyone to use Bayne,' said Philip, 'but needs must when the Devil drives.'

The ground having been covered, indeed rather more than covered by this talk, George was able to speak to Philip of the cottage without embarrassment; whether it was or was not with reserve was more than Philip could judge, but he hoped that Mary had gone far beyond their uncle's intentions.

'I like to have a little place of my own,' George said. 'You remember my little cottage on Dart-i-moor?'

'Do I not!' said Philip. 'You lent it to James and me one long vacation when we were reading hard for Schools. Lovely place.'

'A little too remote and primitive for me at my present time of life,' said George with regret. 'Mary suggests that I should take a cottage here. We'll go and look at it after luncheon.'

Having seen it, Philip agreed that it was very nice, but perhaps too near home to make much of a change?

124

'Oh, the air is very different,' said Mary. 'And it's really in the country. The heath is all very well, but this is the real thing.'

'There are lots of advantages in being near home,' said George. 'Your aunt can get over easily at any time, and I can go over to see them. And I might have Danny here next time your aunts go away.'

Mary looked displeased, but Philip felt entitled to say that he did not think they would care to send the dog to Mrs Simpson again. He related the story of the seance, which seemed safely remote from any dangerous theme and yet not too violent a change of subject.

Mary motored him home, on her way up to London. 'I don't know if I can quite trust you, Philip?' she said.

'You can, as far as I have given my word. Beyond that, I am unbound.'

'I believe you're for the status quo.'

'No, Mary. I'm for a modification of the status quo. I'm earnestly in favour of a better life for Uncle George, but I'm not in favour of a complete uprooting of his present life. It's for him to decide, of course, but I don't see why he shouldn't enjoy his *pied-à-terre* without altogether leaving home.'

'How's the cottage to go on, when he's "at home", as you call it?'

'As the cottage on Dartmoor went on, I suppose.'

'And what about Hilda Twistleton?'

'I suppose she can come in when she's wanted.'

Mary did not pursue the subject, and to his relief said that she had no time to stop for tea.

James was having a brief relaxation between catechism and evensong. 'How did it go?' he asked.

'Well, Mary seems to be doing what I prescribed for her. I'm referred to as "my cousin" – and evidently cast for the role of male confidant, though I rather expect she may soon have to find another. The Twistleton, who adores her, can be the woman friend.'

'Very satisfactory. And your uncle?'

'We'll leave him till after tea. Had a good catechism?'

'Pretty fair. We sang "All Things Bright and Beautiful". I love "the purple-headed mountain" and "the river rushing by".'

'I hope there was no truckling, and that you did not leave out "the rich man in his castle"?'

'Of course not.'

'"The poor man at his gate",' said Philip. 'I always wonder at whose gate, his own or that of the rich man?'

'One of the "ambiguities" critics are so fond of,' said James with a smile.

'You mean Mrs Alexander meant both? I do hope so. I can keep both my pictures – the poor man at a wooden gate to a cottage garden full of hollyhocks and Canterbury bells. Or at the lodge to the castle. He could be the gamekeeper, with kennels full of retriever puppies. But then I'm afraid he might "mess about" – the expression is my aunts' – with the rich man's wife ...'

'Well, we wouldn't tell the children that,' said James. 'I'm sure Mrs Alexander never thought of it.'

18

'Anyhow,' said Philip, 'my aunt's marriage hardly serves its original purpose any more.'

'"The procreation of children",' said James. 'They never had any?'

'Do you know, I'm not absolutely sure? My aunt has always seemed so anxious about the fate of babies who die unbaptized. But I have never liked to ask.'

'I dare say they're quite happy in limbo,' said James.

'Conditions there have no doubt been improved since Dante's visit.'

'And at your uncle's and aunt's time of life they can hardly need "a remedy against sin". But they don't appear to enjoy any more "the mutual society, help, and comfort, that the one ought to have of the other".'

'Indeed they don't.'

'I don't see why they shouldn't live apart then,' said James.

'Aunt Eliza will say it's "setting a bad example". I don't know to whom. To our generation, I think, or to the lower classes. But what they really think is: "What will people say?"'

'At their age it can't "give scandal" to any dangerous extent,' said James. 'Anyhow, I always think too much fuss is made of "scandal". After all, people ought always to think the best. If they don't, it's they who are to blame.'

'It would be ridiculous if poor Uncle George and the Twistleton were thought to give rise to scandal,' said Philip, 'but to gossip they certainly have already. And my aunts will think gossip matters more than it does.'

'I should think your aunt won't care for Twistleton and your uncle to enjoy "mutual society, help, and comfort",' said James. 'It will seem like a reflection on her.'

'But what a mercy it can be enjoyed without marriage,' said Philip, giving him a hug. 'Well, the aunts come back this week, and then the fat will be in the fire.'

'I suppose marriage, however broken down, does give the parties a sort of claim on each other,' said James. 'Though it would be better not to enforce it.'

'Yes, I'm afraid Aunt Jane will think Uncle George owes it to her in some way not to be talked about.'

In spite of his real pleasure at seeing his aunts again, Philip made his first visit to them with some of the guilty feelings of a schoolboy who has been summoned to his housemaster. He had his own faults to answer for, and he was likely to be called even more uncomfortably to account for those of others.

'It was a great pity that you attended Mrs Mullins's seance,' said Eliza almost at once, and closed her mouth remorselessly.

'I'm very sorry,' said Philip. 'The moment I came into the room I saw that I had made a great mistake.'

'It was a great pity,' repeated Eliza.

'I saw I ought not to have accepted her invitation to your house.'

'Yes. And it was a great pity to encourage that sort of nonsense. One doesn't want that sort of person to say that you were there.'

'I'm very sorry indeed.'

'Yes, it was a great pity,' said Eliza, and one could hear her teeth, some of which were strong and artificial, snap.

Jane was even more difficult. 'You went over twice to see your uncle at the hotel. How did you get there?'

'Mary motored me there and back the first time. Miss Twistleton took me there the second time, and Mary drove me back.'

'Was Miss Twistleton there the first time?'

'I didn't see her. Mary was spending a weekend there.'

'You knew Miss Twistleton had established herself there, and had a room at the hotel?' asked Jane accusingly.

'Mary told me so, the second time I went,' said Philip.

'Didn't Kate Springfield tell you long before that? She says she did.'

'She repeated it as a piece of gossip she'd heard,' said Philip. 'I don't know what the foundation was, and I didn't care to inquire.'

'So I might have known nothing about it!'

'I supposed Uncle George would have written to you. In any case we were bound to speak of it when you came back. Will you go over there, or do you expect Uncle George back here first?'

'I've no intention of going there,' said Jane crossly. 'Your uncle can come back, now he says he's so much better – and we've been to all the trouble and expense to make the house more comfortable for him.'

'Yes, the work seems to have been very well done.'

'All the same, I don't quite understand you,' said Jane, unappeased. 'Did they make you promise to say nothing about Miss Twistleton taking charge like that?'

'They didn't,' said Philip. 'But if I had promised, I should of course say nothing.'

'You didn't tell them what you thought about it?'

'No one asked my opinion.'

'But if they had?'

'Then I think I should have tried to say something tactful and non-committal,' said Philip.

'I've no patience with lawyers!' said Jane crossly.

'We have to be careful, you know. One could easily make things worse. And we don't butt in, we wait till we're called.'

'So there's nothing for me to do?'

'There are two things – either you write or telephone to Uncle George and ask when he's coming home, or you wait for him to make a move.'

'Which would you do?'

'I don't know,' said Philip. 'I think only you can decide what is the best thing to do.'

There was a silence. 'What's Miss Tillotson *like*?' said Jane.

'You've seen her,' said Philip. 'On the whole she's seen and not much heard. Very quiet, but if she's excited she bubbles, rather like a kettle boiling.'

'She doesn't sound very attractive,' said Eliza.

'I don't think she is,' said Philip. 'But people seem to find her restful.'

'Do you think she's much attached to your uncle?'

'Mainly as a case,' said Philip, after a moment's thought. 'And a case that she's been very successful with, one must admit. I think the person she's really fond of is Mary.'

'Isn't there anything you can do?'

'No,' said Philip. 'I can't carry messages or do any sort of negotiation. But I won't go over there without telling you first, except in case of an emergency.'

'What emergency could there be?' asked Jane.

'I hope there won't be any. But suppose Uncle George had an attack of some sort and asked for me urgently? But there's another thing – I shall refuse to discuss the situation with Mary. That could do no good.'

'I don't know what she's got to do with it,' said Jane.

'I mean to see she has nothing to do with it, so far as I'm concerned.'

'Maddening not to be able to do anything.'

'But dear Aunt Jane, there's nothing you can do without making a breach that will be difficult to heal. The only definite thing the law can do is to divorce – and you don't want that, and you couldn't if you did.'

'We know there can't be any question of adultery,' said Jane frankly, 'but there's such a thing as desertion.'

'That takes a long time,' said Philip. 'I'm sure Uncle George will be back long before then. But of course you only meant to threaten him, you weren't serious?'

'But aren't there "family councils" and things like that?'

'There isn't any family,' said Philip. 'The two of you must come to an agreement.'

'Oh, if I had anyone to help me!' said Jane, ungratefully.

Philip had a sudden inspiration. 'I wish my mother were here,' he said. And immediately she was there in her sisters' hearts, far more really present than in all Fräulein Schechner's mutterings from Aunt Sibylla's chair. A presence to control and to soften ill temper.

Perhaps she would in fact have solved all problems if she were there, for she certainly had cared for George and Jane and might by now have cared for them more than they did for each other. But death makes a difference; it can fix people or transfigure them in the survivors' feelings. Philip had never had more than a small child's knowledge of his mother – this is greater than is commonly thought, but is necessarily limited. He wondered what his dead relations might have been like if they had lived another twenty-five years. His mother might have become a grumbler or a scold; Ned might be like the odious old men who had once ogled him in a bar at Brighton. The gods had loved them better than that.

'You know, you looked extraordinarily like your mother just now,' said Eliza.

Perhaps her mantle too had fallen upon him.

'Oliver', said James when he went home, 'has turned up again.'

'"Like a bad penny," you seem to say.'

'He's been to see Mrs Dolmidge. "I wish dear Philip would come," she said.'

'I don't feel I can just at present,' said Philip. 'Twice lately I have been a representative of the dead, and a sort of *Deus ex machina*. The first time it was Uncle Ned, and today it was my mother.' And he told James the story. 'So I can't go and be Christopher, or anything like him.'

'Never mind, you'll be able to talk about it to Oliver when he comes to luncheon on Saturday.'

'So you've invited him? I hope Miss Snape will be up to the occasion.'

'I should think so. She can do a mixed grill.'

'And I'll get a good cheese. I don't trust her puddings.'

'Mrs Dolmidge was asking after you,' said Oliver.

'I hope she didn't talk about our last meeting,' said Philip. 'And what have you been up to?'

'"An Unusual Scandinavian Holiday",' he said. 'Frozen seas, the "Russian winter", and a very boring form of skiing, which isn't much more than a country walk with horrid great things on your feet.'

'Why wear them, then?'

'You'd sink into the snow else. And we run a special excursion up to the edge of the Arctic Ocean – all ice, as you might imagine, and covered with snow.'

'How enjoyable! But why do people go?'

'To say they've been, of course.'

'I believe you'd run a cruise to hell if you could,' said Philip.

'It would be a huge success. So far only Dante can say he's been. But at present I'm more concerned with hell on earth – this war, if it's coming.'

'Rather late for you to do much, isn't it? Smart people have gone to America already.'

'Are you doing anything about it?'

'No,' said Philip. 'I can't say I much wish to survive it, if it's going to be all people say. I feel I'd rather perish with Byzantium, so to speak, than try to make a new life in the West, as lots of them did.'

'Of course neither of you could be called up?'

'No, I've got my back,' said Philip. 'I'm what I think they used to call C3. And James has his clergy.'

'That's something,' said Oliver, 'but not very much. There's not going to be a Flanders or Gallipoli this time. I dare say Piccadilly will be the most dangerous place in the world.'

'Well, at least we shan't kill other people,' said James, 'unless by ineffective first aid.'

'What about you, Oliver?' asked Philip.

'Oh, my dear, I'm afraid I may be one of the heroes of the war unless I'm very careful. My firm is working out what we call – between ourselves – an "Operation Funkhole". I may find myself a sort of Scarlet Pimpernel – or is that quite what I mean? – getting people away. We're doing a lot of research, consulting everyone from statesmen to astrologers. Even then we can't guarantee much. I may easily be caught in mid-ocean, or somewhere equally disagreeable.'

The firm was preparing alternative schemes. The first was based on the war being swift and destructive: plans for people getting away while London, Paris and Berlin were destroyed, and Western Europe was swept by gales of gas.

'But people would have to stay away for a while till the mess was cleared up and the bodies were buried,' said Philip gravely. 'There would be horrible diseases, and it would take some time because I don't know who is to do it.'

'Oh, there'd be the Swiss and the Americans and the International Red Cross, don't you think?' said Oliver, and he outlined the 'long-term' scheme. This was to be used if the war went on for years. 'People would have to pay a big deposit,' he said. 'Otherwise I don't know what they'd use for money.'

'I suppose some of them might even earn some?' suggested James.

'Oh, we're going into that,' said Oliver. 'There are embassies and consulates, of course, and British firms and institutions abroad. We are trying to get in touch everywhere, and we might even hint at subsidies. But then, you never know, if the war goes on it will spread, and one has no idea what countries will manage to keep out of it.'

'What is your own choice?'

'Portugal, if I can make it,' said Oliver. 'Nice and cosy.'

'"Some people would be shocked," as Philip's aunts would say,' said James smiling.

'They'd be among the first,' said Philip. 'But good luck to you.'

19

'Lord, I'm sorry for my uncle!' said Philip. 'He's in for a bad time, and I don't see how I can help him.'

'You can't, except by keeping out of it,' said James.

'That I have more or less said to either side. But it's a painful situation. On one side my aunts, who are good, though their cause isn't entirely so. On the other, Mary and the Twistleton whose cause – with some reserve – is good…'

'And you're inclined to think them bad?'

'I don't know. Mary isn't purely actuated by affection for Uncle George – she really hates Aunt Jane. The Twistleton is just in it for what she can get, I imagine. She's probably harmless in herself.'

'What do you think will happen?'

'I rather foresee my uncle caving in, then any advantage he may have gained by this appearance of rebellion won't last long. Back he'll be in that sort of half-life – as Mary quite truly called it – and with no chance of escape. Except, of course, death.'

'But he may take the bit between his teeth,' said James.

'It just could happen, but I think he'd feel rather rootless if there were a real breach. I don't see a very good future for him in either event.'

'Well, Oliver doesn't see much future for any of us.'

Jane's thoughts also seemed, for the moment, to be international. It was perhaps not much for the better, thought Philip, but it made a change.

'If there's a war you and James Freeling would join up, I suppose?' she said, and he really believed it was without irony.

'We should do nothing of the kind,' he said. 'James is a clergyman, and forbidden to bear arms.'

'He could be an army chaplain.'

'He doesn't much care for chaplains and their world.'

'He'd miss his vestments,' said Jane nastily.

'He wouldn't care tuppence about that, but we know in the last war chaplains just had to be hearty and cheerful, and did little to help the dying. There'll be plenty of chaplains. He'll do better work here. If there are raids he can help the dying in this town, if he isn't dying himself.'

'You think it will come to that?'

'It easily could, but I try not to think about it.'

'And what about you?' said Jane, disliking this turn in the subject.

'I'm what used to be called C3, I think,' said Philip. 'My back unfits me for active service.'

'You could have had put it right if you'd done exercises and so on all these years.'

'Possibly, but why should I? It didn't interfere with my work, except from time to time.'

'Aren't you sorry it makes you useless?'

'It only makes me useless as a soldier, and I'm very glad of that. I can be more useful in other ways.'

'What use could your work be?'

'A lot,' said Philip. 'If there's a war there are sure to be lots of tiresome regulations, and I shall have to help people to understand them. Of course, if we're all destroyed in the first few days – as my friend Oliver Hutton expects – it doesn't matter what anyone does. But if it's a long war some sort of life will have to go on. It did last time.'

'But people will have better things to think of than going to law.'

'Worse things, I'm afraid. But the law courts will still have plenty to do, I'm sure. People will get excited, ordinary life will be broken up, girls will be strangled on the heath by Australian soldiers. Don't you remember that at a very critical time in the last war everyone was interested in the trial of George Joseph Smith?'

'You couldn't have been, you were far too young then. And I'm sure I wasn't.'

'I read about it later. But you must have been interested, it's just your thing. Have you forgotten the "Brides-in-the-Bath"?'

'Oh, "Brides-in-the-Bath Smith"! Why didn't you say so first? Of course the newspapers were full of the horrid creature. One thought of nothing else, and quite forgot the war.'

'No one ever quite knew how he'd done it,' said Philip; and they were now set for one of their comfortable talks. Did Smith hypnotize his victims, or what did he do?

However, Jane went back to war. 'Derek is a territorial,' she said.

'Oh yes?' said Philip.

'Won't you feel out of it, not being in uniform?'

'Not in the least. I'd feel wrong in uniform – and I'm not likely to come across a lot of uniformed people here. Luckily one doesn't see Cousin Rosa's horrid sons.'

'They'll look down on you.'

'I really don't care,' said Philip. 'I'm sure they do already. It would take a war to give any importance to such third-rate creatures as the Comstead crowd.'

'I dare say, even with your back, you could get some uniformed office job.'

'Perhaps. Very likely not. People will scramble for them. So stupid – if one's wanted for anything, one will be told what to do. In any case, there won't be a call for millions of men to go and be drowned in the mud by some incompetent general or other. If there's a war, it will be a machine war.'

'So you'd be quite satisfied to go on as you are?' said Jane nastily.

'As far as I can foresee. One can't foresee very far. Really far-sighted people have gone to America.'

'I don't admire them,' said Jane.

'Neither do I "admire" them,' said Philip. 'But I don't condemn them either. People are too prone to criticize their neighbours.'

'You don't think it's people's duty to stick to their own country?'

'Certainly not. Kate Springfield has a perfect right to go to live in Fiesole if it suits her, but she feels she's left it too late.'

'You and James Freeling used to talk of moving.'

'We might have if James had been offered a chaplaincy

somewhere attractive. In the present state of things we're likely to stay put. In better times, if there are any, we shall see.'

'If there's a war, you'll come in for a lot of criticism.'

'I shan't let it upset me.'

'You may get white feathers.'

'Only from very old-fashioned people. Oliver thinks the most dangerous place in the world will be Piccadilly.'

'What does he know about it?'

'As much and as little as anyone else, I imagine. Possibly he has a little more information than most, but it may be untrustworthy.'

'There may be anonymous letters,' said Jane, tossing her head. 'You don't seem to think about exposing us to that.'

'If that's the worst thing any one of us is exposed to we shall be lucky,' said Philip. 'I dare say Bayne will try his hand at one. After all, nothing could suit him better than to harm my credit. I must just rely on you not to help him, and to give me any letters of that sort if they come.'

But then Eliza came in from the town, and her news put an end to their more abstract discussion. She had met Miss Twistleton in the high street. 'Naturally I gave just a curt nod,' said Eliza. 'But she gripped me by the arm. "Unhand me!" I said.'

'Splendid!' said Philip. 'How did you think of that?'

'It just came to me,' said Eliza. 'Then I felt rather sorry because she said quite nicely: "Forgive me, but I did want to have a few words with you, Miss Elwell." One couldn't refuse, and it was awkward to know where to go. One didn't like to suggest going to have coffee, it would seem too friendly – but in the end it was the only thing to do.'

'I would have given her short shrift,' said Jane.

They had gone into a tea-shop, and Miss Twistleton had employed the same opening gambit she had tried on Philip: 'I'm so glad of this chance to talk to you. I know how much Mr Keyworth owes to your sympathy and understanding.'

Eliza had evidently been glum; she was not in Philip's outside position and could not accept any praise that distinguished her from her sister.

'I suppose we shall have my brother-in-law back almost at once,' she had said. 'We've arranged a room for him on the ground floor, as I dare say he may have told you.'

'Ah, that's the point,' Miss Twistleton had said, laying a hand on Eliza's unwilling wrist. 'He's got so much better and stronger. It seems a pity to interrupt his cure so soon. I think the doctor would like him to stay on, at least till the warm weather begins. I felt you would understand.'

'I was more and more uncomfortable,' said Eliza. 'I didn't know what to say to Miss Tillotson. I tried to say that you naturally expected him, Jane. Then I said something, I can't quite remember what, to the effect that she had been rather a long time in attendance on George, and that some people were beginning to find it odd. I tried to sound as if I were saying it for her sake, to warn her.'

'I don't suppose she was a bit grateful for that,' said Philip.

'She was not. "I suppose Kate Springfield has been talking?" she said rudely. "Miss Springfield," I corrected her,' said Eliza. '"I don't see that it matters who it is. It's not very pleasant for my sister."'

Then Miss Twistleton had exploded: 'Your sister calls herself his wife. What sort of a wife has she been? All those years since his mother died he's had no affection or human sympathy. He's just had to feel himself in the way.'

'Miss Tillotson!' Eliza had expostulated. 'I can't listen to this sort of talk' – and it was evident that people at other tables, some of them known to her, were eagerly listening.

'Monstrous!' said Philip, feeling he was no longer pledged to neutrality. 'How can she know about your marriage, Aunt Jane? What right has she to attack you like this? I don't see how any of us can consent to see her again.'

'That wasn't all,' said Eliza. 'She boasted of all she had done for George, nursing him and giving him massage. "Has your sister done half as much?" I said my sister had no need to do things that could be done by paid servants.'

'Magnificent!' said Philip.

'The trouble is,' said Eliza, when she found herself alone with Philip, 'how to go on from there?'

'Yes,' said Philip. 'Of course Uncle George ought to sack the Twistleton at once, for impertinence to you and for insulting Aunt Jane. But I doubt if we could get him to do that just now.'

'We have every right to insist.'

'I quite agree, Aunt Eliza. But it isn't always wise to insist

138

on our rights. We don't give them up, but we bide our time. If she's as violent as that – and I should never have expected it – she'll put a foot wrong somewhere. Then he'll see for himself that she has to go.'

'D'you think she's got him in her clutches?'

'I dare say she might like to – I never thought so before. But I don't think Uncle George would stand for that.'

'So that's how it is,' said Philip.

'I don't see what's to be done,' said James. 'I suppose you couldn't use Doctor Mary as a mediator?'

'I should much rather not approach her. And what would be the good? I must demand the dismissal of Miss Twistleton, and she's Mary's protégée.'

'If you asked for an apology, wouldn't that do?'

'The most difficult thing in the world to get out of anyone.'

'Oh, I don't know. She could write to Miss Elwell that she was very sorry she had flown off the handle and said things she never meant, but she had become nervy at the idea of being gossiped about, when everyone – Miss Elwell first of all – must know there were no grounds for it...'

'That would do perfectly, but who's going to make her write it – unless my uncle does? And the worst of it is that so much of what she said is perfectly true, I'm afraid, though she had no business to say it.'

'I imagine your uncle will know nothing about it.'

'But if he invites me over to see him, I shall have to say that I won't meet her. I do owe my aunts that.'

'Perhaps she may go away for the day – then you could go. And if you could, I think you should.'

'Of course I've no quarrel with him,' said Philip.

'It's all very difficult.'

'No, James, it's impossible. Well, as Mr Pecksniff would say: "That is very soothing." There's nothing to be done.'

20

Philip and Eliza hoped against hope that a penitent letter would come from Miss Twistleton, but no word came. A week later Eliza rang up Philip at his office, urgently calling him to a conference; she had received a letter from George Hamilton Bayne.

My client, Miss Hilda Gertrude Twistleton, has complained to me of the injurious language you used to her on Tuesday 8th March. You suggested impropriety in her relationship with Mr George Keyworth, which you know to be false. You also threw doubt on her professional capacity as a masseuse.

I must warn you that if you make these or other unfounded assertions to the detriment of my client, she will be obliged to bring an action against you for slander.

'This, then, is war,' said Philip.
'But what can I do?'
'Nothing.'
'What am I to say in reply?'
'Well, I suppose even George Hamilton Bayne is entitled to an answer to his letter,' said Philip. 'I think I should say: "Miss Elizabeth Elwell acknowledges receipt of Mr Bayne's letter of 14th March. She has noted the contents." Of course it's absurd to talk of slander. You were speaking face to face with Miss Twistleton, and no one else was there.'
'The other people in the Cadena, but they couldn't have heard every word. It was she who shouted, anyway.'
'I can imagine it. Of course we only talk of the woman between ourselves. She's just trying to frighten us into accepting her. But I'm very sorry, I'm afraid it cuts us off definitely from Uncle George.'

'My dear, I'm afraid your Aunt Jane is more cut up about this than perhaps you think,' said Eliza. 'Of course *I* don't care how long your uncle stays away, but I don't want there to be any silly talk.'

'I'm afraid I'm hardly in love and charity with Hilda Gertrude Twistleton and George Hamilton Bayne,' said Philip.

'Of course you hate their guts,' said James, 'but you love them as a Christian, don't you? That doesn't involve *liking* them.'

'I should be quite pleased if they died.'

'Ah!' said James. 'You don't wish them to die, you only wish them dead — that is, out of the way. If they came into huge fortunes in the Argentine and had to go and live there, that would suit you equally well.'

'Yes, but murderers often only want their victims dead. It's rare for them to hate them. Hatred is the most uncommon motive for murder.'

'Yes,' said James, 'but they usually want something the other man has. They may not be malicious, but they're covetous or jealous. You're neither, and you're not in the least vindictive. You'd never hurt anyone deliberately, and for the sake of hurting.'

'No.'

'That's the beginning of Christian charity.'

'That's a pleasing thought,' said Philip. 'I can't understand revenge. I have to make a "willing suspension of disbelief" when I read Greek tragedy or Elizabethan plays. And I have absolutely no sympathy with people who clamour for it, no matter how badly they've been treated.'

'I think that's a very healthy attitude, even from the purely literary point of view,' said James. 'I'm sure it's better not to identify oneself with the heroes.'

'Yes, "suspension of disbelief" is often the way to read. While reading I can accept the passion of Romeo and Troilus for Juliet or Cressida.'

'You don't change the sex in reading?'

'Never! I don't want to identify myself with Romeo or Troilus or any of the others. I want to look on, and look into them. And I want to extend my experience. Besides, I don't visualize much when I read. I might draw better if I did.'

'Well, to return to the point. If you want a motive for Christian charity, I shouldn't wonder if George Hamilton Bayne and Hilda Gertrude Twistleton didn't draw your aunts together in face of a common enemy.'

'I hope so,' said Philip. 'Life may be happier for Aunt Eliza – and no one deserves it more.'

Indeed there was an atmosphere of peace about the house that was not often felt there. The aunts were living together like sisters in unity, and as their more casual acquaintances may always have imagined them, for they usually put on a united front before strangers. Now they were as polite to each other when only Philip was there as if they were encompassed by their neighbours. Eliza was being more than commonly considerate to Jane, with an almost elder sisterly gentleness that at other times she might have thought excessive. Jane was evidently enjoying the privileged position of being wronged without feeling hurt. Philip cynically said to himself: 'There's little gude aboot the hoose when my gude man's at home.' He, however, felt the absence of his uncle with a real pang, and was rather shocked that Danny seemed perfectly content.

One day old photographs were brought out, Grandma's album to begin with. Many of the people had died long before Philip was born. 'That's Great-Uncle Henry, who ate his eggshells.' 'That's Great-Aunt Mary, who used to crush a sort of stink-bomb when she passed any member of the lower classes in the passage – she didn't like their smell.'

'Sometimes I'm rather afraid I take after her,' said Philip.

'There's your great-grandmother. Once that enormous wig got into a candle-flame. She was bald as an egg without it.'

The sisters both joined in, but the sparkle was Jane's.

'There's your Cousin Rosa in ostrich-feathers. So pretentious of that awful old man, her father, to have her presented. They hoped to get a much grander husband for her than poor Bertie. There was some baronet whose place was quite near Comstead. It couldn't have been one of the Freelings?'

'The ages wouldn't fit,' said Philip. 'Or, yes. Perhaps they might. How lucky she didn't marry James's father.'

'He wouldn't be a clergyman if he were a son of hers,' said

142

Jane. 'Or High Church either. She was always abysmally Low – and she'd have pushed him into the army.'

'Who's this?'

'Oh, that's poor Miss Harcourt-Smithers,' said Jane. 'She'd lost a hand, and had a fork fitted into her wooden arm when she came to dinner with your grandmother – and I must say she plied it vigorously.'

'Don't you remember? When you were a little boy you cried at that story,' said Eliza. 'We had to turn the page quickly.'

'Well, I do think it's rather sad,' said Philip.

'I don't know,' said Jane. 'Someone bravely overcoming a handicap, and eating twice as much as anyone else. It's rather fine.'

'And this man with drooping locks of hair on one side...'

'Your Cousin Eustace. At least I suppose he was a sort of cousin,' said Jane. 'He drank too much, or he had a bad head. He never ventured to join us in the drawing-room after dinner.'

'And the young man in white trousers?'

'Poor Mark!' said Eliza. 'He was drowned in a boating accident.'

'Rather a strange accident,' said Jane. 'In the middle of his uncle's pond. I think he wanted it to appear an accident. After all, he was in trouble.'

'What was his trouble?'

'Oh, never mind that,' Eliza began, but was interrupted by Jane: 'They said he'd been messing about – rather horribly – with a pupil of his. He was being a private tutor during a university vacation.'

'And here's Aunt Sibylla!' said Eliza, triumphantly turning the conversation. And there Aunt Sibylla was, upright and beautiful in her chair, pretending to read a book. There was little meek Aunt Caroline, the widow of a missionary, and the 'plain one'. Grandma, though not a beauty like Aunt Sibylla, was still very distinguished. Grandpa Elwell had a bushy beard, and something like a primitive bowler hat in his hand.

'You've not seen the Hall since you were a small boy,' said Jane. 'Elaine Ratchford asked us to suggest ourselves for tea there one day. Shall we choose a Sunday, and you can come with us?'

The Hall had belonged to Philip's Great-Grandfather

Shrubsole, on whose death, shortly before that of Queen Victoria, it had been bought by people called Goldstein. The heiress of that family had married Fulbert Ratchford.

Philip felt some curiosity to see the Hall again; he was surrounded in his aunts' house by so many things that had come from there. The putative Boucher in their drawing-room, and the authentic bird and flower pictures of the early eighteenth century, had once hung there. And there Aunt Sibylla's throne had had an honoured place. The elaborate gilt clock on the drawing-room chimney-piece, surmounted by a muse holding a harp, had been a golden wedding present to Great-Grandpa Shrubsole and his wife.

And what about Grandpa Elwell? He seemed to have been the ideal Victorian husband and father, energetically occupied in a business that was just not 'ungenteel'. He begat six children, and died leaving Grandma comfortably well off – and in a position to reign matriarchally over the family for more than thirty-five years. His own family never impinged; they were believed to be people of standing of whom one need never be ashamed, but they were in another county. There had been uncles and aunts, and there were still cousins on that side, for Grandpa had been a younger son; but their very names had been forgotten and no one could identify their photographs in the album, if they were there represented. On the other hand every Shrubsole connection was known for the last hundred and fifty years or more. Grandma had evidently behaved to her in-laws exactly as Jane behaved to the Keyworths.

Grandpa probably had no personal interests that had to be sacrificed, nothing to compare with Uncle George's artistic talents. He had further done well by his family by dying in his early sixties – long before his father-in-law Shrubsole – and leaving his widow unencumbered, and able to profit by her father's household. That was what a man was expected to do, Philip thought with a shudder, and he felt all the more thankful that he did not expect to marry.

Philip went to see Miss Springfield, who was due to go to Italy the next week.

'Well, Filippo, what do you think of the situation?' she asked.

'From one point of view I think rather well of it. The aunts have never got on so well together as long as I remember.'

'Yes, there's the foreign enemy to unite them. But they'll get tired of that, you'll find. If they don't argue, what's there to talk about? All the women of that family were the same. You don't remember your grandmother?'

'Only just,' said Philip. 'She once gave me a peppermint cream, and I spat it out on the hearthrug.'

'Well done!' said Kate. 'She and your Great-Aunt Sibylla were just the same. I can just see them walking down one of the asphalt paths across the heath, their two heads together – Sibylla's bent down to a level with your grandmother's – nattering and nattering away. Of course Sibylla, being an old maid like me, thought your grandmother didn't know how to bring up her children. Didn't know how to feed them, I think. Either they didn't get enough meat, or too much.'

'Grandpa died early.'

'Yes,' said Kate. 'He died on retirement. That's what men ought to do in your family unless they have the good luck to be widowers. Then they can live for ever, like old Mr Shrubsole. He had long outlived his wife, and your Great-Aunt Sibylla ruled the roost. He was very old, and so long as no one bothered him, he let her do what she liked.'

'And what she liked was to spend most of her time with her sister?'

'Yes, they're all like that. Jane, when she was a young married woman, and George used to go up to London every day to his office, never took the slightest interest in her own house. She was always over here with her mother and Eliza.'

'But I think she does miss Uncle George in a way.'

'Oh yes, I think she has some affection for poor George – but all mixed up with the sentimental idea that she ought to have more. And a feeling of claim: "He's a poor thing, but my own."'

'Yes, and a justified feeling of hurt about his going off this way without notice, just as they've had the house made more comfortable for him. Why did he do that?'

'Male cowardice,' said Kate. 'He couldn't find anything to say. Anyway he didn't go away, he just stayed away. I expect that that Mary's to blame. I rather think you may have to

145

negotiate with her. There hardly seems to be any other door open, and sooner or later something must be done.'

'Poor Uncle George! But one must try to reserve some freedom for him – though Miss Twistleton will have to go, after her attack on Aunt Jane.'

'Yes, you understand, because you're an artist too – he mustn't just be swallowed up. What a dreadful thing marriage can be! What a mercy that we've escaped it, you and I! At least I have, and I pray you will.'

'Tell me, Donna Caterina, what was my mother really like? For my aunts she's enskied and sainted, and I'd like a more humdrum opinion. Was she like the other women of the family?'

'She was a good deal milder. She was the meek one, like your little Great-Aunt Caroline in the older generation, but rather more intelligent. She was the youngest. Then she was the only woman in the family who had ever been in love with her husband. I can't think why. I know you don't mind my saying this? You never cared much for your father, did you?'

'Not really – perhaps I was matriarchically conditioned, if you see what I mean.'

'All the same, Fanny was happiest and most at ease with her mother and sisters. I think she rather helped to keep the peace, being a bit between Eliza and Jane in temperament.'

'She'd be a help now, I often think.'

'Yes. Being happily married – odd though it seems to me – she understood men better than the others. She was very close to Ned – though Eliza was too in an elder sister way, but Fanny was his own age – and she was very fond of George. A nice woman. You know, her death was the worst thing that has ever happened to Jane?'

'Yes, that comes through. But did you honestly like her?'

'Yes, very much indeed,' said Kate. 'But you know, for all her occasional wickedness, it's Jane who was always my favourite.'

21

'You must be sick of my family,' said Philip.

'No, I like being interested but not involved,' said James. 'It makes me feel almost *sans famille*. We always enjoy watching "the ills ourselves are exempt from"', I'm afraid.'

'But you've really got quite a lot of family.'

'Well, out of sight tends to be out of mind,' said James. 'I like my father very much when I see him. Mother, of course, hasn't much use for me, as I don't play bridge. I'm fond of Aldebert my brother, and his children. The only one I can't stand – apart from distant relations who don't matter – is my sister, Dora. But our dislike is quite mutual, and we don't meet much.'

'What a blessing for you that the place has been sold, and there's no gathering-point for the clan.'

'Yes. Aldebert never invites Dora if I'm going down to stay with him – wouldn't have room for us both, anyway.'

'Perhaps our trouble is being so inbred. Great-Grandpa Shrubsole and his wife were first cousins twice over. I suppose that does make us abnormally conscious of each other, and a good deal detached from other people.'

'St Thomas uses it as one of the arguments against incest,' said James. 'He thinks it would increase family love to an inordinate extent.'

'That's a very optimistic way of looking at it,' said Philip. 'One sees what he had in mind, but I'm afraid it isn't exactly love.'

'Well, let's hope your truce lasts for a bit, though a common enemy isn't the best link between people.'

'No, but in this case there's no danger of the secession of either of my aunts to the wrong side,' said Philip. 'I don't even see how I can negotiate. We must just wait and see, like Asquith.'

'It's beginning to tell on your Aunt Jane,' said Eliza. 'I wish there hadn't been that scene with Miss Tillotson, but I don't see how I could have avoided it. I'm afraid your uncle must have put her up to get Bayne to write that disgraceful letter.'

'I'm not so sure,' said Philip, 'but I don't know how we can find out. I hardly think she'd have dared to do it on her own, but one doesn't know her well enough to say.'

'If it wasn't her idea, whose could it have been but your uncle's?'

'There's Mary,' said Philip. 'I don't trust her an inch, and she quite looks on Miss Twistleton as her protégée.'

'I shouldn't like to think it of her,' said Eliza.

'I don't like to think it of anyone, but it certainly happened. I'd rather think it of her than of Uncle George, because it would make things easier. It's true that if he did it, it would just be because he was in a temper. If it was Mary, it was deliberate nastiness on her part. He wouldn't have thought about the consequences, but she would.'

'What do you think about tackling her?'

'I'm very seriously thinking about it, but I think we'd better wait a bit. I rather expect a move from the other side.'

'Meanwhile your aunt is getting very nervy and difficult,' said Eliza. 'Dr Allchin, of course, is no good whatever. He tells her not to worry, which is ridiculous. It's no good going away anywhere, and anyhow we've only lately come back, as she feels she ought to be on the spot. The other day she had a violent attack of temper, and then her nose bled. I was really afraid it was a stroke and nearly rang you up.'

'I'm sorry Kate Springfield is away. She'd have been a help to you.'

'Yes, good old Kate. But she'd have brought us all the gossip.'

'Poor little dog,' Jane apostrophized Danny. 'Forsaken by his master!'

'He looks very quiet and placid,' said Philip.

'Ah, you don't know him as I do. He goes sniffing about for signs of your uncle. He's very much worried at the rooms'

148

being changed. He can't understand it at all. And of course the downstairs room doesn't smell of your uncle, nor does his own room now.'

'Dear little dog!' said Philip.

'Poor thing, he's sensitive like me, and we're both no longer young. I don't know how we can put an end to this situation.'

'Rather difficult, as long as the woman Twistleton is there.'

'We might insist on your uncle dismissing her.'

'Oh, don't do that!' pleaded Philip. 'That might start endless trouble. She'd say you were trying to do her out of a job – as indeed you would be. I don't know what that ruffian Bayne might not think up. And it might make Uncle George come out in her defence.'

'My dear, I wonder if your Aunt Eliza wasn't unwise to provoke her?'

'Not at all,' said Philip firmly. 'After the way Miss Twistleton spoke about you, Aunt Eliza was absolutely obliged to put her down. None of us can consent to speak to her until she has apologized.'

'But that rather pushed things over the edge.'

'I don't see what else could have happened. Of course Miss Twistleton was angry at being classed as a paid servant, but so she is. If she were not, it would be far worse, far more scandalous. It's there that I see some hope.'

'What hope can there be?'

'We take the line that Uncle George, like a good employer, is loyal to his servants. You know how people won't hear a word against their servants. This is what you say, if anyone is impertinent enough to raise the subject. But you also know that the time may come when people find their servants becoming tyrannical and have to get rid of them. This is often painful and difficult, and they need help. We must be there to help.'

Another time there were complaints against Eliza; she didn't want George to come home. If she had not been so hard on him it was unthinkable he should stay away like this. It had been fatal to their marriage to set up house with her. She wanted everything to go on just as it had done when she and her mother shared the house – no concessions to George.

Philip had to resist the temptation to say that Eliza's patience had done much to keep them together. He did say how anxious she had been to make the house more comfortable for George. If he forgot the fiction that it was Jane who had suggested the change of rooms, he could see that she did not notice.

'Do you think I should suggest going to stay in the forest?' said Jane.

'I hardly think it would be wise,' said Philip. 'There's Miss Twistleton, and one doesn't know how she would behave. It could be very embarrassing.'

'If I just announced that I was coming, she might get out of the way.'

'Or she might not. Don't do it, Aunt Jane.'

Then Jane began to weaken. Was it right, was it Christian to keep up this animosity against Miss Tillotson? Surely good 'church' people like Philip and Eliza must be troubled in their conscience? One ought to forgive.

'We are not out for revenge, we don't want to punish Miss Twistleton,' said Philip. 'That is all that can be asked of us. If she was in difficulties we would help her. If she would make any sort of apology we would let bygones be bygones. We are to forgive as we would be forgiven, and we know we shan't be forgiven unless we are sorry for what we have done, and try to atone for it if possible.'

'Oh, your sort of people will always have an answer for everything,' said Jane impatiently. 'Always the letter of the law, not the spirit.'

'I have no idea what you mean,' said Philip. 'But I do think the problem of forgiveness is rather difficult. The people in the Gospels are always asking to have their debts forgiven. They only ask for patience, and they are so sorry that one would be a brute to refuse them. I think other words are needed, somehow, when one is talking about people who are quite impenitent, and indeed rather pleased with themselves. I think we are only asked to be without rancour or vindictiveness, and *ready* to forgive.'

'Then there's nothing to be done,' said Jane. 'But how can that Tillotson woman know we're ready to forgive her? Those Oxford Groupists would say we ought to tell her.'

'Nothing could be more foolish,' said Philip. 'People hate being forgiven unless they've asked for it. She'd ask what she was to be forgiven for. And one wouldn't copy those vulgar

150

Groupists in any way. Odious to use the name of Oxford for anything not first rate, like the marmalade.'

Rather to his surprise Philip seemed to have calmed her down, and another period of quiet ensued. If you visited Jane and Eliza, as Philip sometimes did between tea and dinner, you found a scene of peace. Whether it was a day when they had a fire in the drawing-room, or whether it was in the upstairs sitting-room, they were sitting quietly, as Philip had so often affectionately and enviously pictured them when he was away at school, or in his father's chilly and unwelcoming house. Jane was probably unpicking or altering some garment; Eliza might be occupied with her endless tatting, her feet raised and precariously balanced on a little stool. Or they were reading their library books, with the tickets fluttering at the end of the string. There would be no cross voices unless they were impersonally levelled at Eliza's wireless, which was reporting the results of debates or conferences.

'Talk, talk, talk!' Jane would exclaim, though one hardly knew what else she thought the talkers ought to do.

Then a letter came.

My dear Philip,
    Isn't it time to break the ice. Why don't you go over to luncheon with Uncle George one Sunday, as soon as possible? He's dying to see you, and of course there's no quarrel between you and him. I rather wonder you haven't suggested yourself before now, but I can imagine you may have been waiting for a word from him. He rang me up to ask to write. If you decide to go the Sunday after next I will pick you up as I shall be going too. Looking forward to seeing you. Let me have a line.

With love,
Mary

'This requires a careful answer,' said Philip. 'I shall show you that first draft, James.'

'You'll need to make a rough draft?'

'Yes, I must have a copy in case I want to show it to the aunts later on. I think my letter will be rather less cordial.'

'So I imagined.'

Trying to collect his thoughts, Philip began, as a moralist might have advised him, by thinking of his affection for George, which went back as far as he could remember. This was the one man of the older generation who had treated him with tenderness and imagination when he was a child and his own father had been bored and cold. Even George's occasional mistakes were on the side of the angels. He himself had suffered at Charterhouse, and with tears in his eyes he had besought Gilbert not to send a delicate, nervy boy like Philip to a public school. Philip in fact was sufficiently stoical to get through his first year there without traumatic consequences, and he was clever enough to be too high up in the school to be in any danger of ill-treatment ever after. Nevertheless, though he was glad that George's advice had not been followed, he loved him the more for having given it. Jane, of course, had thought it 'great nonsense', and had said so. 'It did a boy no harm to be knocked about' – she would not have said the same of a horse or a dog.

Thereafter George had followed his academic successes with pride, generously rejoicing at being outstripped intellectually. He had been equally generous in encouraging Philip's drawing, which he knew to be better than his own, and in urging the boy to make art his life work. At home he had never shown any resentment when Philip was treated as the pampered son of the house, while he was neglected and made of no account. How could Philip act against him if he were now trying to make life a little more agreeable for himself? And yet, how could he give approval to the woman who had so insulted his aunts?

He wrote his letter.

Dear Mary,

Thank you for your letter. Of course I miss Uncle George intensely, and long to see him. But the matter has become sadly complicated. I cannot meet Miss Twistleton after all she has said, until she apologizes to my aunts. I dare say she was taken aback when my Aunt Eliza warned her (most kindly) that she was getting talked about. I am sure this was only meant as a caution – but people dislike cautions and one can forgive her for her very unpleasant reactions. If she had sent an apology, my aunt would at once have agreed to forget the episode; instead she had the effrontery to get her solicitor to write a ridiculous letter. Even now I am sure the matter could be patched up, and I very much hope you will do this good work.

Meanwhile, should Miss Twistleton be absent or (as I hope) have ceased to live on top of Uncle George – cannot he manage with occasional massage now he is so much better? (but of course you must be the best judge of this) – I shall be glad to go with you on any Sunday, at a day or two's notice.

Yours ever,
Philip Milsom

'A good letter, I think,' said James. 'Conciliatory, but erfectly loyal to your aunts. We'll see what Doctor Mary has ⊃ say to that.'
This is what she said.

Dear Philip,

I am disappointed to find you so easily influenced, but I suppose I ought to have been prepared for it. Miss Elwell must have given you a very misleading account of her insulting words to Hilda Twistleton, who had hoped for a friendly talk with her. Poor Hilda was so taken aback that, most unfortunately, she opened her mouth about Aunt Jane – and as you would say in your affected way, *toute vérité n'est pas bonne à dire*.

When she went back to the hotel she was in tears and in such a state that, in spite of her devotion to Uncle George, she was anxious to throw up the job. Fortunately he got me on the telephone, and I was able to persuade her to stay at her post. She has been his good angel, and the loss of her would put him back terribly. She's not just 'any paid servant', as your aunt called her – words on which it is kinder not to comment. As she was naturally anxious to be protected against such a scene occurring again, Uncle George dictated a letter for her to send to Bayne. Of course there was no intention to bring an action for slander, but merely to scare your aunts into decency.

I shall keep your letter to myself, so that you can come

with me to see Uncle George without hesitation. Hilda is very forgiving, and in any case won't visit the sins of the aunts on the nephew. And I know I can trust you always to be quite the little gentleman.

Yours sincerely,
Mary Keyworth

'Phew!' said James. '"Kinder not to comment". I suppose she thinks that's a kind comment?'

'I don't know what to do now. Those young people who argue about the world situation in the pubs and clubs would think it absurd that I should let this storm in a teacup so distress me.'

'They would, but I have discovered that they are often very unkind to their parents – in my parish at all events. If charity doesn't begin at home it seldom begins at all – and people who keep a "social conscience" often don't feel they need bother about any other.'

'I think there are real moral problems here,' said Philip, 'and that they are always important and even interesting.'

'Yes, at one time I don't think people ever said: "But all *this* is so trivial, when *that* is happening".'

'Because they didn't know that *that* was happening. It's the newspapers that have given people this false sense of proportion, and that soothingly false sense of responsibility for things they can do nothing about.'

'I know,' said James. 'It's much more fun to feel responsible for something that doesn't call for action on one's own part. Once I was so much distressed by a crisis in the newspapers that I forgot a duty of my own – a meeting or something. So I set myself the penance of not looking at the papers for a week, and an axious week it was too.'

'Our young friends would have thought the penance more sinful than the omission,' said Philip. 'But I'm not sure what I can do about this. There is so much truth in what Mary says – there are faults on both sides and some merits too. Uncle George is trying to keep real freedom, and Aunt Jane isn't just trying to save her face. The only person who is faultless is Aunt Eliza, and even she must have contributed in the past to the building up of this impossible situation.'

'If you don't want to give up in despair, or at any rate not yet, I can only think of one move you can make,' said James.

'What's that?'

'Try to arrange a meeting with Mary on neutral ground.'

'I had been thinking of that. I might go up to London, to show goodwill.'

'I should,' said James. 'Take an umbrella with you, like Chamberlain, as an emblem of peaceful intentions.'

22

'I have to go up to London some time about the Grampian–Stokes matter,' said Philip. 'I'll ring up Mary, give her a choice of days, and ask her to have luncheon with me.'

'Where will you take her?'

'Probably I shan't *take* her, but meet her at the restaurant. What would you recommend?'

'Nothing heating, no curry of course. An Italian restaurant?'

'No, pasta requires undivided attention. We want the sort of business luncheon food that people fork into their mouths between snatches of argument. But it ought to be good. The ambience is even more important, somewhere quiet and comfortable.'

'Try Chez Jean-Yves.'

'A good idea. Of course she'll have to choose her own menu, but she may be a bit guided by me. If she isn't, and chooses something bony or mouth-filling and gives me the advantage, it will be her own fault.'

'If you've time, why not ring up my mama and have a cup of tea with her afterwards?' said James. 'She likes these attentions.'

'But what about the bridge?'

'Oh, you'll have to get away before that to catch your train.'

'Well, here goes then,' said Philip, taking up the telephone. 'Yes,' he said to James, 'Doctor Mary was very gracious. You'd think she positively liked the idea of coming out to luncheon. She chose Tuesday and is to meet me at Chez Jean-Yves. She quite agreed that we needed to have a talk. She sent you her regards.'

'You can give her mine when you see her.'

'And you'll dispense me from the Lenten fast? After all, I shall be "travelling".'

'Of course, and you'll have exhausting work too, I'm afraid.'

'I expect so, and anyhow it won't be an occasion for lentil soup or a poached egg, will it?'

'Today I saw Miss Tillotson in the town,' said Jane.

'Awkward for you,' said Philip.

'Not at all,' said Jane, tossing her head. 'It would have been a great deal more awkward for her if we had spoken.'

'You don't mean you cut her?' said Philip, surprised.

'Of course not. But I'm far-sighted, as you know. I see people coming from a long way off, and turn my steps accordingly.' And she gave one of her charming, wicked smiles. 'I think I caught sight of your uncle, too, in the Cadena. I suppose she'd put him there to wait for her. I decided not to go in, and went to the Pandolfinis instead. Their coffee is just as good.'

'I wonder what they were up to,' said Eliza.

'No good, I should think,' said Jane. 'Or George really could have come here to see us, if it was only for Danny's sake.'

'Dear little dog!' responded Philip ritually. 'By the way, Aunt Jane, I have to go up to London on Tuesday for the day. Is there anything I can do for you or Aunt Eliza?'

'No thank you, my dear, I don't think so,' they both said.

'And I'm afraid I can't do anything for them,' said Philip to James.

'No, it's rather a forlorn hope,' said James. 'But you must be as optimistic as possible. What are you going to take to read in the train?'

'I've got the Grampian–Stokes dossier, of course,' said Philip. 'But it's not very exciting, and I know it by heart. I think I shall just do a crossword puzzle.'

'A very good idea. And for coming back?'

'I shall pick up something at the station bookstall. Better not to have a book with me, it might distract the conversation.'

On the chosen morning Philip was ready to go to the station just as James got back from church.

'I said mass for your intention,' said James.

'Thank you, my dear,' said Philip. 'After all, my intention is peacemaking. Do I look suitably dressed?'

'Suitably, yes,' said James. 'Thank heaven you could never look "smart". Of course, if you were really Chamberlain, your umbrella would be neatly furled.'

'I can never manage that,' said Philip. 'But I'm sure there'll be a few drops of rain to justify its being floppy.'

Drops of rain there were in plenty, as he made his way to the Stokes' solicitor. There, as usual, he was very well received, and after business was done he asked for a candid opinion about Bayne. 'Dodson and Fogg' was the simple answer.

Reassured (though he hardly needed to be) by the classification of Baynes among the worst attorneys who had ever disgraced the profession, Philip went out into yet more rain. He disliked London very much, and always seemed to have spare time there at an hour when and place where there was nothing much to do; too late to go to the National Gallery if he were to be in time for Mary in Soho, as he must be. There was nothing for it but to buy another newspaper and settle down to have coffee in the cosiest shop nearby.

Finally, arriving in Soho, he went into St Patrick's for what James called a 'mouthful of prayer', for the success (if it might be) of his mission, and at all events for patience.

'Doctor Mary looked very neat and efficient,' he told James that evening. 'But a strange distraction happened while we were still drinking our sherry. Oliver came in with an important-looking couple – stage people, I think.'

'You'd think he would have gone somewhere more chic,' said James.

'Yes, you could see they thought they were slumming. I suppose someone had told them Jean-Yves was "amusing". Oliver waved at me patronizingly. Of course it was quite good enough for me.'

'I should think so. If he'd gone further he would probably have fared worse.'

'Yes, but he'd have been seen by more important people than us. Mary was quite impressed, and asked me lots of questions about him. She even suggested that I ought to be more like him – how one's female connections love the lowest when they see it!'

'Beware of spiritual pride, my dear!' said James, smiling. 'Oliver has got something we haven't got, let's face it. Not perhaps anything good or bad in itself, but it could be used for good.'

'What's the answer to this riddle?'

'Well, he has a certain toughness – you know I don't like him – but I won't yield to the temptation of calling it crassness. And I think he's got more of what he would call "guts".'

'And what would you call it?'

'"Guts", I'm afraid. I can't find any other single word to cover it.'

'Anyway, he started Doctor Mary off on a discourse – it was rather familiar on her part, I thought, though not really to be resented. She found a new way of telling me I was my own worst enemy. "You see, you're too timid, too humble," she said. "Of course we all know you're like that! But tell me, has anyone ever made you suffer for it? Of course not. It's you who have been too cautious and self-effacing. You've punished yourself for something you know isn't a crime."'

'Do you know, I almost begin to like Doctor Mary?' said James. 'Oliver, of course, is neither cautious nor self-effacing.'

'Well, I told her all that wasn't the whole of life, or even a very big part of it, and that she was too intelligent to be crudely Freudian. And if I was naturally self-effacing, and for lots of reasons, why shouldn't I be? I didn't want to be extrovert like Oliver. This only gave her the opportunity for another attack. It was my family that may partly have made me like this – but I stopped her before she could pitch into them.'

'She must have been having a good time. You were a successful host.'

'A bit too much so. I thanked her for giving me a free consultation, but said it was time we got down to brass tacks. We'd finished our smoked salmon.'

'What did you have next?'

'I'd ordered *crêpes de volaille*, and after a little thought Mary followed my example. We had quite a good hock.'

'Very nice and suitable.'

'"You're not an emissary from your aunts?"' she asked. I told her that they did not know I was meeting her. I didn't want to raise their hopes in any way. "Better so," she said, rather grimly. That made me afraid I wasn't going to do much good. So I put my elbows firmly on the table, and said: "I'm going to be quite frank with you. I'm out for a compromise."'

'I suppose she could hardly say she wasn't?'

'No, people always say they are, even if it means they intend to get ninety-nine per cent of what they want. I said I wanted my uncle to be officially domiciled in his home, but to be free to have a *pied-à-terre* elsewhere. Mary countered this by saying he had signed a contract for the cottage, but she graciously said he might go home as much as he liked.'

Then the vexed question of Miss Twistleton came up. Mary reproached Philip for trying to make a scapegoat of the woman, to push her out, and then to negotiate a peace between their uncle and aunt. This, of course, was very much what he wanted to do, though he would have used other words for it. It was, he thought, the right solution. It need not be done unfairly or in a hurry; she could be compensated, and given time to find another job.

'Why should she be victimized because of a lot of old women's gossip?' asked Mary.

That, Philip said, was not the chief reason for getting rid of her. She had been intolerably rude about Jane to Eliza, and she wouldn't apologize.

Much of what had already been said or written was said again, and more than once.

'We seemed to have been there an intolerable time,' said Philip. 'One could understand why people smoke continuously on such occasions – filthy habit, but it must somehow fill gaps Mary and I had to leave unfilled.'

'Have you noticed how novelists, when they're at a loss, make their characters smoke incessantly, to make us think they're doing something?' said James.

'Yes, indeed,' said Philip. 'I have often wanted someone to examine some of the novels of the baser sort. I think it would be found that over six hundred words, that is nearly one per cent, are taken up with the ignition, consumption and extinguishing of cigarettes. Entirely useless. It tells nothing about character.'

Philip and Mary, who had not that addiction, could only have numerous cups of coffee. Being both intellectuals, and in the habit of working in the afternoon, they shunned the sleep-inducing effect of liqueurs.

'I don't think Uncle George will easily let Hilda go,' said Mary. 'He has lately made a new will, and I imagine she is to be a principal legatee.'

'Then I hope she won't poison him,' said Philip kindly.

Mary looked explosive, hardly knowing whether to have a burst of rage or of laughter. Fortunately she chose the second alternative.

'So that's why Uncle George was in town the other day,' said Philip. 'He must have gone to visit Dodson and Fogg about his will.'

'Dodson and Fogg?' said Mary in a puzzled voice. 'He goes to Bayne and Bootle.'

'I've always thought it a slander against your sex to say that women don't read Dickens,' said Philip, 'but I see you don't. Well, it's never too late to begin.'

'Dickens?'

'Yes, Dodson and Fogg are the attorneys in the *Pickwick Papers*, the foulest in the profession. I nickname Bayne that. Of course Bootle, if he exists, may be quite a good sort of person.'

Then Mary had appealed to him not to forsake his uncle altogether. George was so fond of him, and now he felt cut off from everyone.

'If Miss Twistleton were to go, I'd go and see him at once,' said Philip.

'Must you take up your aunts' quarrels?' said Mary.

'It's very difficult,' said Philip. 'I can't go over to see Uncle George without telling Aunt Jane.' Then he had a sudden inspiration. 'I'll go if she asks me to go. I think one day that may happen.'

There they had to leave things.

Philip wandered into the Charing Cross Road and found a shop where he could turn over old illustrated books. He still wanted a model for Henry James's Maisie. She must not be Pre-Raphaelite, she must not be George du Maurier, she must not remind people of Alice. He had filled his notebook with sketches, but he would not despair. Who knows but the face he wanted might be opposite him in the train one day?

'As for your mother's tea, James, I won't torment you with an account of it in Lent,' said Philip.

'I know what it must have been.'

'She was quite anxious about you, and hoped "poor Jimmy" wasn't overdoing the fast.'

'Well, I'll tell you how we can give her pleasure. We can ask her to send us one of her cook's plum cakes. Really it is I who should have sent her something for Mothering Sunday. It will keep well, and we can have it on Sundays, if we're ever in to tea.'

'Splendid, if it doesn't offend Miss Snape.'

'No, "her ladyship" can do anything she likes with her. But what are you going to tell your aunts about the luncheon with Doctor Mary?'

'Nothing, I think, as nothing really came of it.'

'But why are you looking so cock-a-hoop?'

'I saw Maisie in the train, her very self – and with the old governess too! I've got them down, I'll show you. No one could guess *What Maisie Knew*!'

23

Philip surveyed their Lenten breakfast table. 'How depressing this meal would be if we hadn't got a really good coffee machine,' he said.

'Yes, indeed,' said James. 'You don't look as if you'd slept well.'

'I haven't,' said Philip. 'I'm beginning to think that after all I had better tell my aunts about yesterday. There's no harm, we know, in *suppressio veri*, but the truth won't always stay suppressed. Then come the complications.'

'Yes. "Why didn't you tell us?" people say. Then *suggestio falsi* comes in, as it's difficult to make a civil answer that is truthful.'

'I don't think it would be in my case. Aunt Eliza's forensic gifts would only get the truth out of me, but it might be uncomfortable. I think I'll have to tell them about Uncle George's cottage, as it must come out soon – and while I'm about it I may as well mention his visit to Dodson and Fogg, don't you think?'

'Yes. I find that very disquieting.'

'You mean the Twistleton now has a motive for poisoning him?'

'No,' said James, smiling. 'It would be a little too obvious, wouldn't it? I meant, are there reasons to be afraid that your uncle is becoming senile? Is he completely under her thumb?'

'You know, I've been worrying about that,' said Philip. 'That letter from Dodson and Fogg to my aunt first gave me the idea. There seemed to be a sort of senile rage about it, exploited by George Hamilton Bayne. If he's got like that, and he's not old enough for it yet, things are pretty hopeless.'

'You'll want to go and see for yourself.'

'Yes, but I'll keep my word to Doctor Mary. I think I can

get Aunt Jane to ask me to go. It's odd, isn't it, that Mary didn't touch on that point? She's a geriatrician, after all.'

'Perhaps she's besotted with the Twistleton. Perhaps she wants to see you again to give you another talking-to. Anyhow, you didn't ask her.'

'You can understand that, James. I have a sort of horror of mental weakness. I look away from it if I can. In any case I couldn't talk of senile decay in Uncle George, to whom I'm devoted, except impersonally in a doctor's consulting-room, or to people I'm fond of. Not to Doctor Mary in a restaurant.'

'There's so little to be done about it, too,' said James. 'You might one day be able to contest your uncle's new will, but I don't suppose your aunt thinks about that.'

'Only negatively, I should think. She wouldn't want the Twistleton to get anything, of course.'

'Will you suggest to her that he may be senile?'

'Not directly. I may get her to suggest it to me, and then we can talk about it. That would make her want me to go and see him.'

Meanwhile they were planning short holidays. Sometime in Easter week James intended to make his annual visit to his brother in Devonshire. Philip would go to Rome rather earlier, and might look in on old Kate Springfield in Florence on the way.

'Devonshire cream and pasta,' said Philip. 'Just what we need to regain any weight we may have lost in Lent.'

'And sunshine too, I hope.'

'And escape from problems, public and private,' said Philip.

'How "some people" would disapprove of that sentiment, at least of the first part of it!'

'I always wonder how "some people" manage,' said Philip. 'Granted that they read two newspapers every day and two weeklies every week and argue about them, but what do they do for relaxation? Observably they have never read anything worth reading, unless it was forced on them in youth, for exams.'

'I shall never understand them,' said James. 'I hardly need to, for they seldom require my services, except to bury them.'

'People are fond of saying that "the Church is out of date", but whose fault is that? It's an ancient and respectable institution and, like Milsom and Dolmidge, doesn't need to tout for clients.'

'I suppose they think one should write letters to the press or talk on the wireless,' said James. 'They're so hopelessly out of touch with reality, though it's the last thing they think they are. Somewhere I read an article by an imbecile who invited the Church to neglect theology and philosophy in favour of "reality". What could he mean? Theology and philosophy!'

'I don't think they would think much of my absorption in a private problem,' said Philip. 'It's only concerned with personal relations and the happiness of two or three people. Well, I shall be able to talk about it on my holiday with old Kate. Otherwise I shall leave Tuscany and Umbria for our journey in July.'

'So you saw Mary when you were in town,' said Jane. 'Why didn't you tell us before that you were going to?'

'I thought it better not to seem to be a messenger from you,' said Philip. 'And I didn't want you to worry about it beforehand.'

'What did you get out of her?'

'Nothing satisfactory,' he said, and he told her about the cottage and the visit to "Dodson and Fogg".

'She's got your uncle under her thumb,' said Jane. 'But if I know him, that won't last for ever.'

Philip was much surprised.

'You'll see,' said Jane. 'There'll be a reaction. We'll just leave it for a time. Perhaps you might go over and look at things when you get back from your holiday.'

Not displeased at this reprieve, Philip was able to devote most of his free time and his thought to Maisie. That strange little face, neither pretty nor plain, seemed to say exactly what Henry James wanted it to say, and bafflingly no more. The other characters had already been fixed and the work would be done before he went away.

He was with Kate Springfield for a few hours in Florence. She had come down from Fiesole and they were drinking coffee in an 'English tea-room', which was not very like the Cadena or even Pandolfinis. Nevertheless it was raining.

165

'Wet enough to give us "Home Thoughts from Abroad",' said Kate. 'I wonder how poor old Musso is without me.'

'I rang him up – or rather, Florrie – the day before yesterday, and got a good account,' said Philip.

'That was a kind thing to do!' said Kate. 'How few men would think of doing such a thing!'

'Aunt Jane was almost shocked when I told her. Men should have more important things to think of.'

'Dear muddled soul!' said Kate. '"Real men" like your father, or that dreadful Comstead lot. She doesn't like them, and she certainly didn't marry one.'

Philip gave her the complete up-to-date history of what she called 'l'affaire Twistleton'.

'Do you know, I shouldn't wonder if Jane was right,' she said. 'George is capable of temporary infatuations. I don't suppose you ever heard of Phyllis Thompson?'

'No, indeed.'

'You were still quite small. It really became very awkward. That horrible brother of his, Norman, put his oar in and made it much worse. Norman even tried to make poor George emigrate, and arrange a separation, and he had the impertinence to tell Jane that it was the best thing for her. She soon put him in his place. She was absolutely loyal to George – I think the tie between them is stronger than anyone imagines, themselves included.'

'The interesting things you tell me, Caterina!'

'Well, no one else who can would,' she said. 'I think his mind will clear, and then will be the chance to oust the Twistleton.'

'Let's hope so.'

'We must wait and see, like Mr Asquith. We can afford not to be in a hurry. Twistleton can't poison him so soon after his will has been made,' she chuckled. 'And what about you, Philip? Are you here on the hunt for Henry Jamesy people?'

'Not specially, but if any suitable Italo-American types turn up, I shall try to take a note of them. I don't suppose you have any at your pensione?'

'Oh dear no! It's not a place for American merchant-princesses, as Henry James quaintly called them. How one loves him even when he's absurd! It's for nice English middle-class spinsters like me – the sort of people Florence was built for, one feels – certainly Fiesole.'

'Just as Venice was built for American tourists, though I suppose nice children must always like it.'

'Yes. And you can tell your friend the Church will always have a future as a tourist attraction, whatever the nasty press says – Rome, and the English cathedrals.... What's Father Freeling up to, by the way?'

'He's going to spend a few days in Devonshire with his brother after Easter. Meanwhile he'll be busy hearing confessions, I should think.'

'Shut up in a box?'

'No, we don't have confessionals at St Simon's – "too Roman". George Hamilton Bayne would be on the rampage at once. James just sits in a Windsor chair, and the penitent kneels on a prie-dieu at the side.'

'More hygienic for him, but also more embarrassing.'

'I shouldn't think he had anything very shocking to hear. People who do shocking things seldom confess them, I fancy.'

'Except in public, if they join those horrid vulgar Groupists – like my cook. Not that her pastry is any the lighter for it.'

In Rome Philip was utterly happy: lovely things to see, and just enough time or money, no responsibilities (for Dolmidge was looking after the office, and letters were not forwarded) and, so far as he was aware, there was no one he knew nearer than old Kate in Fiesole. But once entering the Caffè Greco, he saw Oliver at a table with important-looking people. He waved amicably and retreated, for he supposed that Oliver's beckoning gesture was not meant to be regarded as serious. It even gave a further interest to his days to dodge all that party, little as they were likely to have wanted him.

Finally he ran into Oliver in a travel office.

'You ought to have come in and joined us,' said Oliver. 'Larborough asked me who you were. I could see he was rather attracted.'

'The attraction wasn't mutual,' said Philip.

'Tut! You'll never better yourself,' said Oliver. 'Now I

suppose you are going home to the Reverend James and the other aunties?'

'Exactly.'

'And you're quite contented?'

'Certainly, except that I hate leaving Rome.'

'Perhaps it's really better to be like you,' said Oliver almost ruefully. 'I dare say you escape a lot of worry.'

'All I can.'

He returned home to find his rooms swept and garnished, perhaps a little too clean, as they smelt of cleanliness and did not feel very cosy. And as usual when one lives closely with a dear companion and looks forward to a short absence on his part as a time for tidying up bits of work, he found it a disappointment. He was not in a working mood, and merely wanted his friend to come back.

'"But that also is very soothing,"' he said, quoting Mr Pecksniff to himself. It would be sad not to wish for James's return. And he rang up Devonshire.

'Philip?' said Aldebert's friendly voice. 'Bertie here. Jimmy is in the garden and little Alethea is trying to teach him to play croquet, so she thinks. Was it all right in Italy? You weren't bothered by the Albanian affair, I hope? Jimmy will be back with you before next Sunday. He's spiked the church here up as High as it will go. He's sent off three tins of cream, for you, your aunts, and Miss Snape. You should get it tomorrow. But next time you must come here too.'

So the following afternoon he went to bring his aunts their Devonshire cream.

'How sweet of James!' said Jane, for the first time taking this liberty.

Otherwise his aunts were a little difficult. They seemed to think that Philip was not to be left alone for a moment, and ought to eat almost every meal at their house during his friend's absence. 'The women of your family are like that,' he remembered George saying. 'If you want to do anything on your own, they'll tell you you're neglecting your work, but if they want you for anything, your work can go hang.'

However, they were again living in peace and unity.

'But I think', said Jane, 'it would be rather a good thing if you were to go over and see your uncle – just to see how he is, you know.'

'Without any programme?' said Philip. 'Yes, I shall. I think I'll telephone Mary to see if she will arrange it. Better she should drive me there, if she will, rather than the Twistleton. It would be embarrassing to be alone with the Twistleton for six miles. Besides, Mary may persuade her to get out of the way.'

Oliver rang up, and came in for a drink.

'So here we are again. Where's James?'

Philip told him, and asked where he himself was staying.

'Out at Andhurst, with Larborough,' he said. 'You needn't turn up your nose.'

'I didn't mean to.'

'I suppose you can't help your reactions, but they don't really suit you. Who are you, after all?'

'Nobody.'

'I wouldn't quite say that, my dear. You're Milsom and Dolmidge, so you're somebody in this town and for quite a wide radius around. But you could be a good deal more if you chose. What you've inherited or got by education is not a bad basis to build on, but not very much in itself. You've not got a place, or a title, and you're not heir to anything. It's not likely you'll ever be a world authority on any subject that's much in vogue. You draw prettily, but any more closed cul-de-sac than illustrating Henry James...! My dear, who reads him? You're quite amusing at times, but you can't hope to be a wit when you've no one to talk to but James and your aunts.'

'You want me to have a dose of "London talk", I can see.'

'I suppose you're envious of it, or you wouldn't pretend to despise it.'

'I neither despise it nor envy it. If I wanted it, I'd go and have some. I don't necessarily despise something I don't want for myself, such as a yacht or a fine stamp collection.'

'Even living here, you could contribute to the weeklies – you used to be quite bright. Then I dare say you'd soon be invited to broadcast. But you should buy a car. Think of the difference it would make to your social life! You must have some smart clients, an old-established firm like yours. And your own connections in the county are quite good, and

James's are better. If only you cultivated your twenty-mile radius to start with...'

'I might dine with four and twenty families, like Mrs Bennet.'

But Oliver did not remember who Mrs Bennet was.

'You', said Philip, 'are like old Major Pendennis, with a dash of my connection Mary Keyworth thrown in.'

'But one might as well talk to a stone wall,' said Oliver. 'You used to be much more fun. You won't come over while I'm with Larborough?'

'Not even to see all those yards of red and blue morocco.'

'It's not even as if you were a leftist,' said Oliver. 'Some of them are quite smart. *They* aren't so haughty about Larborough's invitations either, let me tell you.'

24

Philip made arrangements with Mary for a visit to their uncle. 'No, I'm not climbing down,' he said firmly. 'I'm doing exactly what I said to you in London. Aunt Jane has asked me to go, and I'm very glad to do so. If you are kind enough to take me one Sunday I shall be very grateful.'

'You don't sound it.'

'Oh, sorry, Mary. I'm not good on the telephone. But I do want to see Uncle George.'

Then George rang up.

'I'll be delighted to see you, old boy. You and Mary had better lunch with me at the hotel, and so Hilda Twistleton will be free to go off and see her cousins.'

Evidently things were to be made easy for him. He asked his uncle if there was anything he would like brought from the town. George said he was rather badly off for books, and asked if Philip could supply him with some detective stories. He remembered that he had a stock of them.

'And we'll go and look for more,' Philip said to James. 'Luckily detective stories are usually "nice". My uncle doesn't like books to be "beastly" or "unnecessary" any more than the aunts do.'

'What's his usual reading?'

'Surtees, I think. He probably likes Trollope too. Aunt Eliza is the only one who likes Dickens, I'm afraid.'

Mary duly appeared, smiling amiably but rather smugly as if she were making up a quarrel or receiving back a prodigal. But she didn't matter, and Philip resisted the temptation to point out that he had done nothing that required forgiveness. They talked quite easily, for the six miles, about Italy.

'It's good to see you, Phil, old boy,' said George.

Mary had left them alone for a moment, and George went on: 'I wish we could talk comfortably, without these women about. At home, your aunts weren't on top of us at every moment. Now Hilda's there all the time, only rather unwillingly went off for the day, entrusting me to Mary.'

'Well, I'm obliged to Mary for the lift,' said Philip.

'Oh, I expect I could arrange for someone from the hotel to pick you up another time,' said George. 'Some of them go into the town to church. I'm sure I ought to be grateful to Hilda, who has done so much for me and still does. A bit too much, if you ask me. Never realized that she was such a large woman. She takes up such a lot of room in the cottage, and I hear her heavy tread whenever she moves about. There's still no talk of her finding rooms or whatever she wants in the town, and all these weeks have gone by. I don't know how to give her a hint. Old Emma looks after me perfectly, and I don't need a sort of nanny – too old for it, and not quite old enough yet.'

Mary appeared, and they went into luncheon and made innocuous conversation. Philip's trip to Italy was no use as a theme; George was the sort of person who liked saying that England was good enough for him. However, he was quite interested to hear that James had been in Devonshire, though not on 'Dart-i-moor'. 'Aldebert Freeling,' he repeated. 'Nice to hear the old name again, I'm glad they keep it up. But lucky for him the place is sold. Ghastly to have to come in for that white elephant – if I may call your school that, Mary.'

'I should think so,' she said. 'Hideous pile. The ugliest house in the county, and nearly the biggest.'

'Comstead is ugly enough too,' said Philip, 'though nothing like the size. I wonder how they're all getting on without Cousin Rosa.'

'Going to the dogs, I believe,' said George with satisfaction. 'Poor Bertie is up to his ears in debt. I shouldn't wonder if they had to sell the place, but the Lord knows who'd buy it.'

Then for Mary's sake there was some Keyworth conversation, with George mainly at the receiving end, as he maintained little contact with his brothers. The dangerous name of Hilda Twistleton was not mentioned.

However, when they went over to the cottage, Mary withdrew into the kitchen for a chat with old Emma. She was

172

almost obviously giving George and Philip the chance to talk to each other without her. George promptly took advantage of this. He was just a little rambling, a little repetitive, but he seemed to be very much all there. Again he spoke of the Twistleton's size and weight.

'Stumping up the stairs, bursting into rooms so that the furniture shakes. Looming over me and fussing. And then she's always suffering from Hurt Feelings – Lord, how tiresome! Though she looks as if she had the hide of a rhinoceros. She weeps or she rages, she gets really violent, and I'm afraid she's going to break a blood vessel or something. But Mary discovered her, and won't hear a word against her.'

Mary came back, and talk returned to matters that interested none of them, but just before it was time to leave she slipped away again.

'Now the weather's warmer I feel very like going home,' said George. 'I don't need to be under the doctor's eye the whole time, and I want to see your aunts and old Danny.'

'Dear little dog!' responded Philip.

'Yes, I certainly must go back soon,' said George. 'You might drop a hint, next time you go to see them. I'll ring you up from the hotel one day.'

'Uncle George, we must be going,' said Mary, who had gathered up her bag and scarf. 'By the way, what's happened to that nice lustre jug you had on your bureau?'

'Hilda broke it, clumsy cow, barging about,' said George. 'She's too large for the cottage, and such a weight.'

'All the better to massage you with!' said Mary.

Again by common consent Philip and Mary avoided awkward subjects. He left her to go to his rooms, not wishing to give her ocular confirmation of what she no doubt suspected, that he was going straight to report to his aunts.

He telephoned, and Jane replied: 'Yes, my dear, do come. Kate Springfield is just back and is here. Imagine, she wants to go and stay for a few days at the Forest Hotel, while her bathroom geyser is being mended!'

'A very good idea! Do keep her till I come.'

'Aunt Jane doesn't like that at all,' he told James. 'As a family, we all love to keep our friends and relations away from each other.'

173

'I've noticed it, even you aren't free from this trait. What's the reason for it?'

'I think we're afraid they'll talk about us behind our backs.'

'Of course they will,' said James. 'But that's not always harmful.'

'In this case it may even do good,' said Philip. 'I think old Kate is just what my uncle needs — someone to talk to out of his own world. She'll be very fair-minded too, though of course she's a partisan. Besides, she's never even met the Twistleton, though Aunt Eliza once urged her to employ the woman.'

'How did you find your uncle?' asked Jane.

'Pretty well,' said Philip. 'I think you'll be seeing him fairly soon.'

'You didn't see Miss Tillotson, I hope?' said Eliza almost accusingly.

'No, I think she'd been sent out of the way on purpose. I gather Uncle George finds her rather a trial. He couldn't say much because Mary was there. She appointed Miss Twistleton and he says she won't hear a word against her.'

'Well, you'll know some more soon,' said Kate Springfield. 'I'm going to stay for a few days at the hotel while my geyser is being done. George will talk to me.'

'If those women let him,' said Eliza discouragingly.

'Oh, I'm sure Uncle George is quite often on his own,' said Philip. 'He asked me to bring him a supply of detective stories, and he must have time for reading. Miss Twistleton has other patients, you know, so she can't be there every minute. He's pretty tired of her by now, and he'll be delighted to see you, Caterina.'

'But they'll think you came from us,' said Jane.

'Do I look as if I came from anybody?' said Kate. 'I shall talk about my geyser, and I shall say that Philip gave a good account of the hotel. That's why I'm going, anyhow. I have to be out of my house, and as I've just been abroad it's natural I shouldn't want to travel farther.'

Then she attacked Philip. He ought to stand for the Town Council. One wanted more gentlefolk on it, people who would consider the interests of old-established residents and not just tradespeople wanting to make the town bigger and uglier, and with vain ambitions to revive it as a tourist resort. Ridiculous winter gardens and recreation grounds and that sort of thing, when we had all played on the heath as children. If it was good enough for us, it was good enough for the children of today. But anything to put up the rates!

Philip demurred. He said he was not cut out for any form of public life.

'That's just what our sort of people always say,' said Kate. 'We don't want to put ourselves forward, we can't be bothered. And for us, of course, it's no honour to hold some potty little office. But what happens in consequence? We're just leaving the place open for bounders like George Hamilton Bayne.'

'Kate is rather fond of laying down the law,' said Jane, after Miss Springfield had gone. 'But she's quite right. We do need some people of the right sort on the Town Council. You ought to stand.'

'I hope Father Freeling isn't too socialistic to approve of someone on the right side,' said Eliza. 'He wouldn't approve of the extravagance of those people who want to put up our rates?'

'No,' said Philip, 'he'd be all for better housing, but he wouldn't want money wasted on winter gardens, and all that sort of nonsense.'

'All that talk about "progress", it makes me so cross,' said Eliza.

'It isn't "progress",' said Philip. 'It's the most reactionary thing possible to try to make the town into a resort again. It hasn't been one for more than a hundred years. Now, people don't come any more to drink the waters.'

'Thank goodness we're not on the sea,' said Jane. 'At least they can't bring the sea here and build rows of cabins and a pier.'

'That's beyond the powers of even George Hamilton Bayne.'

'You'll have to smarten yourself up,' said Eliza. 'And it would help if you got married.'

'No, I'm not going to alter my life to please the Town Council,' said Philip. 'If I stand, they must take me as I am, or not at all.'

175

'All the same, I don't really like Kate going to the hotel,' said Jane, who had been brooding. 'She wouldn't want to make mischief, but you never know. She might make some joke and upset everything.'

'Her sense of humour is under control,' said Philip. 'She intends to be diplomatic, and I think she will be. But, as she said, she'll be very independent. She won't be your ambassadress.'

'Real humour is always kind,' said Jane, 'but Kate's isn't.'

'I couldn't disagree with you more,' said Philip. 'Real humour can be very cruel, but Kate wouldn't sacrifice her friends to a joke.'

'In some ways I envy you for being a priest,' said Philip. 'You have to forget what people tell you in confession. You've trained yourself not to brood over their worries. And you can pray for them. That is action.'

'True,' said James. 'But nothing prevents you from praying yourself. And if you imagine that people keep their worries for confession only . . .'

'Yes, but you can give advice without impertinence. You even get asked for it. I have to be very cautious.'

'That's no bad thing, but I admit you are more exposed to receiving advice.'

'Yes, indeed. Now they want me to stand for the Town Council.'

'That might be no bad thing either. The presence of an intelligent person in any crowd is probably an advantage. You ought to be glad if you're called on a jury. You would make it a little more likely that justice would be done.'

'That's what I think. Of course they want me to keep the rates down.'

'Well, there's a lot of extravagance on the Council. You could try to check that, without prejudice to necessary things like housing.'

'I shall wait until someone invites me. Then, perhaps, I ought to accept. But I don't see why I should go touting for nomination.'

'I entirely agree with you. *Pace* our progressive young friends, I don't think one commits a sin of omission unless one neglects a really obvious duty – even a command in most cases.'

'What fun they would have if they went to confession. "Since my last confession I omitted to attend such-and-such protest meetings. I didn't vote on such-and-such occasions." Some of them would be capable of adding that so many million people had died of "warre, dearth, agues, tyrannies". So jolly to accuse oneself of what one couldn't help.'

'I should say: "You must confess a real sin of your own, or I can't absolve you. Did you go to mass on Sunday? Were you snappish with your husband at breakfast this morning?"'

'One would almost be tempted to tell them to go out and commit a sin.'

'Unnecessary. They're probably in a chronic state of ill temper and of envy too.'

'Ah, well, we can leave them for just now – and leave my uncle too, though I rather expect to be summoned to his help quite soon. He will hardly be able to escape unaided.'

'Then you'll have all the "action" you can desire – and a bit more, I should think,' said James.

25

'It's hard not to worry at times,' said Philip. 'Though one fights against it. Alas, as a family we're rather addicted to it. Aunt Jane even goes so far as to pride herself on it.'

'At least I can try to convince you that you shouldn't,' said James. 'It seems to me that almost the only original contribution of Christianity to ethics is the lesson not to worry, and to be humble. Other things may be more important, but they have been said before.'

'But there's a new crisis coming. Kate Springfield is back from the forest and wants me to go and see her without the aunts' knowing.'

'Well, there's nothing to worry about till you hear what she says, and most likely there'll be nothing then.'

In fact what she had to say was sensational.

'George is terrified of the Twistleton,' said Kate. 'I suspect you of having been very naughty, Philip! Did you know that several of the books you brought him are about nurses murdering their patients.'

'Good gracious!'

'I quite expect him to send for you to save him.'

There was one alarming book about a nursing home in a Midlands town, and it was hinted that it had a basis in truth. The proprietress, a sinister person called Nurse Wellington, gained an uncanny power over her female patients. Some of these had made their homes with her and had engaged to leave her all they had in return for special treatment and slightly reduced fees. They were not young, but it was remarkable how early they became senile, and then 'Nurse' kept them severely from their friends and relations. The mortality among them was high. Another line of 'Nurse's' was stillborn babies. When she came up for trial, someone swore he had heard a father say: 'The child will be born dead, of course.'

'The child's father?' asked Philip. 'Like Byron.'

'No, he had departed and left no address,' said Kate. 'The girl's father.'

It appeared that the patients had died easy deaths, and to that extent 'Nurse' had been a benefactress. But the friends and family of her victims had suffered cruel procrastinations, promises to be allowed a visit next day, and the visit postponed again and again. Finally one niece disputed her aunt's will, because some family heirlooms had been left to 'Nurse', while it had always been understood that the niece was to have them in reversion. This chink of light shed on the nursing home widened until 'Nurse' was arrested and had to stand trial.

'She was strung up, I'm glad to say,' said Kate.

'And in real life?'

'I think so. I'm almost sure of it, though the fools of jurors recommended her to mercy. I suppose she was a handsome woman, and was lucky enough to have no women on the jury.'

'She must have been more engaging than the Twistleton.'

'Yes, that great galumphing creature,' said Kate.

Then she went on to another case. This was the subject of a famous and blood-chilling novel. The villainess killed by injecting air-bubbles into vital arteries, her only weapon an empty syringe and the only trace a harmless looking spot. 'I expect it's frequently done,' said Kate comfortably.

Perhaps, but one could imagine George haunted by this spectre of the lady with the needle. The merest, most innocent seeming prick might be murderous.

There were more criminous nurses in the detective stories. One of them was in league with the doctor, who would naturally be ready to sign the death certificate.

'Of course it's rubbish,' said Kate. 'Poison wouldn't be the weapon of a great, heavy, clumsy woman like that. However, I didn't want to reassure George too much, as we do want him to get rid of her.'

'He ought to give her notice.'

'There's a lot against that,' said Kate. 'To begin with, he wouldn't dare. His courage has been sapped. And then she'd make an appalling scene – bellowing like a rhinoceros. Do rhinoceroses bellow?'

'I expect so. And of course if things were brought to a head like that, Uncle George might have reason to be frightened. She would have to act quickly or not at all. He might fear that she'd break his neck, as she easily could.'

'I know. One doesn't know how to arrange his escape. He could just abscond, and leave a letter for the Twistleton, but one doesn't like that.'

They finally arrived at a sort of compromise. George should leave openly on a visit to his home, and then should stay away. It was very much the way in which he had settled into the hotel and then the cottage. Philip's office should deal with Miss Twistleton, and old Emma could pack up George's things and forward them.

'I'll prepare your aunts,' said Kate. 'The essential thing is that they must be ready for him at any time.'

'That's where they'll make difficulties.'

'Eliza will be so middle class,' complained Kate, 'fussing about the parlourmaid's afternoon out, or the day the laundry comes back.'

'But it will be easier to persuade her than Aunt Jane that the matter is urgent. What excuse is Uncle George to give for his visit?'

'We won't say that anyone is ill. I share your superstition about that. But we can quite truthfully say that Danny is beginning to feel his age.'

'Dear little dog!' responded Philip. 'I know, I'll make a surprise visit after the office one evening. I'll hire a car.'

'No need for surprise. Telephone to the hotel the day before. Then you can have a quiet talk with George, and arrange to fetch him later.'

'Then he can write from home to dismiss the Twistleton. He'll tell her that she can apply to my office for compensation in lieu of notice, but I expect she'll go in a rage to George Hamilton Bayne.'

'I'm afraid you'll have to see one or other of those beauties,' said Kate. 'And I dare say Mary Keyworth will want a word with you as well.'

'"What will be shall be,"' said Philip with resignation.

Two evenings later he went out in a hired car. George was

waiting for him at the hotel and seemed overjoyed to see him, but Philip was grieved to see him looking old and shaky.

'Kate Springfield didn't think you were quite so well,' said Philip. 'She seemed to think you'd do better for a little time at home, so I thought I'd come to see what you felt about it.'

'Yes, take me away, Phil,' pleaded George. 'Take me before that woman has done me in.'

There appeared to be no use in reasoning with him, Philip simply let him talk. George had convinced himself that he was being slowly poisoned and he had imaginatively induced some of the symptoms. Philip's only care was that their talk should not be overheard. He proposed the Springfield plan. 'I'll come out on Sunday. I'll hire a car again. Don't say anything about it till an hour or two before. Then say that you have to meet me here for luncheon, to talk over family business. Have a little bag ready in case you find that you need to come back with me. The rest is up to me.'

Everything went according to plan, but after luncheon George said, 'I think it would be more civil if I just looked in at the cottage to tell Hilda I'm going back with you. I shall say it may be for a few days – to gain time.'

'Then what will happen? D'you think she'll ring up?'

'I hardly think she'd dare ring up your aunts' house. She might try your office, I suppose.'

'That would almost be an admission of defeat,' said Philip. 'I don't think she'd care for me to know that she wasn't in touch with you. I think we'd better send her a letter in three days' time. Give you time to see Henville-Poke and for any other arrangements.'

'Oh, my will?' said George. 'I shall just cancel the last one. I made it in a bad temper. Your office has the old one, and that will come into force.'

'Not for a very long time, let's hope,' said Philip.

'The new one would have been proved jolly soon,' said George cynically. 'Hilda would have feathered her nest.'

'I hope not, but anyway she won't now. Do you want me to see her?'

'Not specially. But if you have to, you'll say as little as possible?'

'It can just be a formal greeting.'

And so it was.

181

'Keep well, Mr Keyworth,' she called out. 'Bring him back soon, Mr Milsom.'

At home they were all very cosy. Kate Springfield was there, and they were going to have dining-room tea. Eliza had seen to it that there was toast and Gentleman's Relish for George (the others preferred scones and honey) and a pot of black Indian tea for him and Kate. She had even had a large breakfast cup put out for him, though Jane grumbled that it did not match the others.

Gradually George's nerve was restored; a visit from Henville-Poke next day, and a subsequent examination, revealed that he was not suffering from arsenical poison, and the symptoms induced by fear quickly disappeared. George Hamilton Bayne returned his copy of the new will, and, after its prompt destruction, if anyone had a motive to kill George it was not Hilda Gertrude Twistleton. Nevertheless the maids had been instructed that no one would be at home to her if she called.

'Danny will bite her,' said George. 'Dear little dog!' Though poor old Danny seemed past any aggressive action.

Philip had to write the uncomfortable letter. Perhaps it was cowardly of George to put this task upon him, but he felt inclined to indulge his uncle as far as he could. He tried out phrases. 'My uncle, Mr Keyworth, asks me to write for him ... my uncle wants me to say ... he particularly wishes to express his gratitude to you for all you have done for him ... he finds that he wishes to spend some time at home now ... his doctor, though much impressed by his progress, feels that he should rest from massage for some little time, and likes to have him under his eye.... Mr Keyworth of course wishes not only to make up your salary to date, but to compensate you for lack of notice.... He seems, for various reasons, to feel that a meeting between you at the moment would be inadvisable and agitating.'

'I bet it would!' said James. 'But you can't tell her he thought she wanted to poison him.'

'I'm afraid I can't tell Mary that either. I'll go on: "If you care to write to me at my office, or to call by appointment, I shall be pleased to discuss any further business that arises." I shall hate it, but after all it's the sort of thing I'm there for.'

'You realize that they'll say that you carried off your uncle and are holding him prisoner?' said James.

'I think Hilda Gertrude can hardly say that to anyone but Mary, or George Hamilton Bayne. Anyhow, I don't quite see how we can stop it.'

'You can't, in your uncle's present state of mind.'

'It doesn't matter, so long as it doesn't come round to my aunts and upset them.'

'No, but you'll have to be careful,' said James. 'How long do you think the present situation is going to last? And what will happen if your uncle wants to go to the cottage for some days? Is he fit to go by himself?'

'I'm not at all comfortable about things,' said Philip. 'I helped him to get rid of the Twistleton because he really wished it, and in the interests of peace at home. What next? I suppose he could go and stay in the hotel again from time to time if he wants a change. He's aged rather. I don't quite see him on his own.'

'There's a person to see you, Mr Philip,' announced Miss Snape a few days later. Miss Twistleton had turned up too late at the office and had followed him home.

'What name?'

'Miss Twistleton, I think,' said Miss Snape. 'A very strange person. Not the sort of person I think your aunties would care for you to receive. I wouldn't like to say for sure, but I think she's been drinking.'

'I had better see her, Miss Snape, otherwise I think she might trouble my aunts.'

'Oh, that would never do!'

'Would you stay at hand?' said Philip, knowing that this would give her exquisite pleasure.

'Lord, give me patience!' he prayed. Then he saw charity also was needed.

'Do sit down, Miss Twistleton.'

'I must see Mr Keyworth,' she said. She had not been drinking, but was in a state of great excitement.

'One moment. Let me have some coffee brought you.'

'I don't want anything.'

'But I want you to have something. You need to relax a little. Miss Snape makes very good coffee.'

He went to the door and gave an order.

'You're keeping my patient from me!' she cried.

'Now, just a moment.... For the time being I think it much better for you and Mr Keyworth not to meet ... I hope you won't insist on it ... I know how good you've been to him, and for him.... But you know elderly people get fancies ... I expect you've already found life difficult with him from time to time.... Just now he'd rather not see you...'

'I don't believe you. It's a conspiracy with your aunts.'

'Let's leave my aunts out of it, shall we? Let us confine ourselves to you and Mr Keyworth. I'm here to help you, if I can.'

'I don't believe you.'

'In that case, I'm afraid I can't talk to you. I don't talk to people who don't believe me. Shall I leave you to drink your coffee, and then ask Miss Snape to send the maid to show you out? Is that what you want?'

'No, I'm sorry. I was hasty.'

'Very well. Now you know Mr Keyworth is rather nervy, don't you? ... Can't you feel that in a way it's a good thing that you should be honourably released from your duties? ... You must sometimes have asked yourself if you could hang on.... I don't need to tell you that you will be properly compensated ... and if you want a reference you can apply to me as well as to Doctor Mary...'

'I was going to consult my solicitors – Mr Keyworth's, I mean.'

'My firm now deals with Mr Keyworth's business. Of course you have the right to consult anyone you like, but you can consult us for nothing. Come to my office, if you will, any morning when you're in town, as I shall have the papers there. You won't lose by it. If we don't satisfy you, you will still have the right to go elsewhere. But I own I'd rather we kept the matter to ourselves, and I think it may be better for you as well.'

'I think you mean to be kind.'

'I mean to be just,' said Philip, in case she was stupid enough to resent kindness as an insult. 'Doctor Mary knows all about old people from the outside,' he went on. 'But

184

sometimes I wonder if she knows them from inside. She's as strong as a horse, and I should think she's never had an illness in her life – and with all her qualities, I don't think she has much imagination. Now, we know a bit more. You've nursed someone you were close to for years – your poor mother. And I have always been close to Mr Keyworth and that household. Besides, at one time I was a crock myself. You and I know how hard life is for people who can't move without pain – difficult to pick something up from the floor, impossible to get something that has rolled under your bed...'

'Yes, and to have to work out your movements,' she replied.

'Yes, indeed, almost like a ballet dancer. This must influence the mind. It becomes painful to make any decisions or to have any arguments. I really think it would hurt Mr Keyworth if you insisted on seeing him just now. I wish you would leave it for a time, and then you can meet as old friends. Will you think about it?'

'I'll think about it. When shall I call at your office?'

They fixed a day, and she retreated in better order than that in which she had arrived.

Philip was exhausted. 'Will you ask Father James to come to my room when he gets back?' he asked Miss Snape. 'I shan't want any supper – just some soup, if you have any.'

'So virtue went out of you?' said James.

'I hope enough to settle the business, but there's still Mary.'

He waited for Mary to write, and so she did.

I don't know if you have gone back on us, Philip, and to tell you the truth I don't much mind. Uncle George seems now to need hospital care more than anything we discussed. I don't feel like going to see him in his present domestic bliss, and I don't give it long either. Hilda says you've behaved like a gentleman.

Uncle George sent for me to take him home (wrote Philip, which was about as near as he could get to the truth without unsuitable explanations). It was his own idea, and I don't see what else I could have done. When he's a bit settled, James and I mean to have an early holiday in Italy.

185

Perhaps we may meet after our return, if you find yourself this way? At the moment I don't think we have much to say to each other.

'That is more or less true, isn't it James?'
'You can't do better without mentioning the detective stories,' said James with a smile.

26

James and Philip went to Umbria.

'This may be our last civilized journey,' said Philip. 'Let's miss out Assisi. Sure to be full of English spinsters studying what they call "things Franciscan".'

'But you adore Kate Springfield.'

'She won't be there, and she'd say "Franciscan things" if she talked about them. We'll get away from everything. I haven't even given anyone a poste restante.'

This sort of liberty is paid for by anxiety on one's return, not that any return is without it. Who was the French writer who could not come home after even a few hours' absence without fear of being met with dreadful news of his wife and family? Later, in the cruel years that followed, those who lived through them had to learn to keep such fears at bay. Now in a period still civilized, Philip could feel really comfortable only when he went to bed at home. James would be in his room across the passage, and Philip would have telephoned to his aunts at the latest hour they permitted. Anything that might happen to anyone else, any black-edged envelopes in tomorrow's post or deaths in *The Times* could, even if it were with sorrow, be endured. But he wished to be 'tough' with his fears, and not to fuss his companion from one poste restante to another, and therefore had forsworn communication with home during the journey.

The letters waiting for him when they got back did not look ominous, but when he telephoned to his aunts he learned that George had had a stroke and had gone into a nursing home – one that was happily above suspicion. Meanwhile Danny had died peacefully of old age in his basket, and had been buried in his pink blanket under a lavender bush.

'I'm sorry I wasn't there,' he said.

'Oh, my dear, what could you have done?' said Eliza. 'I'm glad we couldn't spoil your holiday by writing. It was best like this, and your return was something for us to look forward to. Besides, you were very good about sending postcards.'

He felt some doubt if Jane would be equally generous, and she was not.

'Most inconsiderate!' she said. 'Didn't you want to know what was going on at home?'

'I hoped it could wait,' said Philip. 'It's all right waiting for news. What is dreadfully tiresome is when letters get mislaid – as they do when you don't quite know your programme.'

'We always get our letters when we go abroad.'

'Yes, but you go to one spot. We were travelling to see places. We like to be free from dates, so that we can spend extra days at a place we like, or leave a place we don't like at once.'

'Very happy-go-lucky,' said Jane with disapproval. 'I wonder James isn't more responsible.'

'Why should he be? His one obligation was to be back by a fixed day, and so he was. There are other clergy at St Simon's, and old Dolmidge could look after my clients.'

'You won't be able to travel like this when you've a family of your own.'

'Another reason against having a family of my own.'

'Selfish!'

'No harm in thinking of oneself when there's no one else one is obliged to be thinking of. After all, we're all trained to be self-reliant, self-controlled and self-respecting.'

'Not to be self-indulgent,' said Jane sharply.

'But if one never indulged oneself a little, one would never be indulgent to other people,' said Philip. 'One wouldn't know how, and they do need it.'

'Tcha!' said Jane. 'Soon they won't be able to be.'

She had always had an almost puritan objection to the small indulgences of other people, particularly those of the 'lower orders' – which did not prevent her making very kind presents to the maids from time to time.

She had long had a particular aversion to Sunday cinema.

'But it's somewhere to go, something for them to do,' said Philip.

'Let them save their money,' said Jane. And nowadays she was even opposed to the entertainments of their 'betters' as well. Soon everyone would have to get down to work – war would come and would make total demands on everyone. The government, fools though they were, would clamp down on every form of organized pleasure.

'They'll be fools if they do,' said Philip. 'People won't think so much sacrifice is worthwhile.'

'We get on without all those amusements.'

'Because we're fortunate, and have homes of our own and people in them,' said Philip. 'We're not the sort of people who care about bars and expensive restaurants and cinemas and theatres and the palais de danse. But we have our own indulgences – light and warmth and books and music and everything done for us that we need without our lifting a finger. I'm not going to criticize people who spend their free time differently.'

'You sound almost socialistic.'

'I'm not at all,' said Philip. 'I want people to be better off, but I don't believe that a system is going to do that for them. After all, there's a sort of equality in prison and in schools. I dare say it isn't hard to make people more or less equally miserable. You can't make them equally happy. And I couldn't bear a world where all the corners were rubbed off, and there was no room for individuality or eccentricity.'

'You'd be eccentric anywhere,' said Jane.

George, who was believed to be out of danger, died in his sleep while the world was still agonizing in its last hopes of peace.

'*Felix opportunitate mortis*, I'm afraid,' said James. 'He rests from his labours. But it's a grief for you, Philip, and labour too, I fear.'

'Aunt Eliza and I are the executors,' said Philip. 'The old will comes into force, and there shouldn't be any difficulty there. But how is Aunt Jane going to take it?'

At first she went to pieces, as if she and George had been the most devoted couple in the world. She could not be expected to do anything, she must be treated as an invalid; let Philip and Eliza arrange everything that had to be arranged. She was not to be worried; she would see nobody!

'All very well,' said Eliza to Philip, 'but when she feels a little more used to the situation, she'll find fault with everything we've done.'

A new problem was raised when they found that George had left an envelope with instructions in addition to his will. He wished to be cremated and that his ashes should be scattered.

'This is odd,' said Eliza. 'George always hated the idea of cremation. I suppose he really wished it?'

'We have to act on it as if he did,' said Philip. 'I think I can guess his reasons. One can't be cremated unless a second doctor signs the death certificate. George must have thought of this when he was afraid of being poisoned.'

'He had plenty of time afterwards to tear it up,' said Eliza. 'I wonder why he didn't.'

'I expect he got used to the idea,' said Philip. 'I'll telephone to the crematorium at Bromsbridge and ask them to arrange a day and time.'

'Then your aunt will say we should have disregarded it.'

'It's Uncle George's wishes that we're responsible for,' said Philip. 'And there's one great advantage for Aunt Jane. If there were an ordinary funeral she'd have to have some of the Keyworths to tea or luncheon. Now they'll drive straight to Bromsgrove, and go home afterwards. I shall notify them, of course, and that will be all.'

'I'm afraid your Aunt Jane won't come,' said Eliza.

'I don't think she need, to a cremation,' said Philip. 'You and I can take a car, and perhaps Kate will come with us.'

'How extraordinary not to consult me!' said Jane at the first opportunity. 'I don't at all like the idea of cremation.'

'Aunt Eliza and I have to carry out Uncle George's wishes,' said Philip. 'We're his executors.'

'How do you know he really wished this at the last?'

'We have it in his writing. He would have destroyed it if he had changed his mind.'

190

'I can't go,' said Jane. 'I don't think women should go to cremations.'

'I must,' said Eliza. 'I'm his executor, and I want to show my respect to the last.'

'I don't want to be left alone then,' said Jane. 'And there might be an air raid at any time. You'd better stay, and we'll read the service together. Are you taking a clergyman with you, Philip?'

'The chaplain at Bromsgrove does things very nicely,' said Philip. 'I've had to go two or three times for other clients. James offered to come and take the service, but I didn't want to have him there with all the Keyworths – they'd have tried to get hold of us.'

'Quite right,' said Kate Springfield. 'But you must have someone with you. We can't appear to be giving George up completely to the other side.'

'"The other side",' said Jane. 'What a way to talk of my husband's family!'

'I meant no harm,' said Kate. 'I shall come with you, Philip, and I think Eliza certainly should. You can spend the morning quietly in bed, Jane. It's a great thing Bromsgrove is a few miles away. There will only be family there.'

'Thank goodness you and Aunt Eliza were here,' said Philip.

'Yes, how could you have faced all those people alone?' said Kate.

'"Uncles Stanley and Norman, Aunts Eileen and Dawn",' said Philip acidly. 'Not to speak of Derek and the Honourable Molly!'

'Mary at least didn't come,' said Eliza. 'But she sent quite a nice, simple wreath.'

'A contrast to those terrible "floral tributes",' said Philip. 'I wish we had said "no flowers". But Mary did right, I think. She was giving Uncle George back to us.'

Kate insisted on Philip's stopping to have coffee with her in the town, while Eliza was driven home.

'The last time we did this was that wet day in Florence,' said Philip.

'What years ago it seems!' said Kate. 'And now I wonder if we'll ever get back there again.'

'It's something to live for.'

'A good thing to have,' said Kate. 'It may keep one alive. And now poor Jane is telling Eliza that she has no one left to care for her.'

'She wouldn't count you and me,' said Philip.

'No, and certainly not Eliza.'

'Poor Aunt Eliza – if it comes, she's going to have a dreadful war.'